The Heroic Female Spirit

The Heroic Female Spirit

A Collection of Tales

by
Phyllis K. Peterson

Bahá'í
PUBLISHING

WILMETTE, ILLINOIS

Bahá'í Publishing
415 Linden Avenue, Wilmette, Illinois 60091-2844

09 08 07 06   4 3 2 1

Library of Congress Cataloging-in-Publication Data
Peterson, Phyllis, 1941–
    The heroic female spirit : a collection of tales /
by Phyllis K. Peterson.
        p. cm.
    ISBN-13: 978-1-931847-29-2 (acid-free paper)
    ISBN-10: 1-931847-29-0 (acid-free paper)
     I. Title.

PS3616.E847H47 2006
813'.6—dc22

                                              2006042703

Cover design by Tracy Heckel of gutentag.us
Book design by Patrick Falso

Contents

Acknowledgments

I am continually reminded that authors are only as good as their editors, and the work that my editors have done is absolutely profound. I credit senior editor and director of acquisitions, Terry Cassiday, and editor Alex McGee for taking my good stories and making them great stories. Others who have also read the manuscript and offered a few suggestions are Christopher Martin and Bahhaj Taherzadeh. Thank you one and all for helping this book to achieve its true purpose! I also wish to thank Lee Minnerly, general manager of the Bahá'í Publishing Trust, for his support in this endeavor.

There is one woman who has helped me to have faith that I could be courageous in the face of adversity, and that is my mother. Single-handedly she held our family together. While she is in the advanced stages of Alzheimer's disease, she continues to be my hero.

And finally, I wish to thank my children who helped me to believe that I could be an author. I dedicate this book to them.

Introduction

Stories and storytelling have always influenced people's view of themselves and the society they inhabit. As the author of *The Healing Power of Stories,* Daniel Taylor, writes, "It is not surprising that the bulk of moral education in human history has been through models, exempla, heroes—that is, through story."*

And just as our culture has stories, so do we also each create a narrative of our own lives through a story of our self: "The construction of the individual's story will be influenced by the dominant stories of the culture, but which of these stories are chosen . . . and which roles in the stories are identified with, will contribute to the ultimate uniqueness of each individual's life story. Both existing stories and stories newly constructed provide meaning to life. It is by living in and through the chosen and constructed story that life becomes meaningful."†

When the stories of our culture cause someone to be neglected or diminished as a person, as has happened with women and girls, it has a corresponding effect on

---

* Daniel Taylor, *The Healing Power of Stories: Creating Yourself Through the Stories of Your Life* (New York: Doubleday, 1996), p. 46.
† Phebe Cramer, *Storytelling, Narrative, and the Thematic Apperception Test* (New York: Guilford Publications, 2004), p. 4.

identity, self-worth, and confidence. Instead of being portrayed as heroic, women are depicted as weak and passive, either residing in the background or waiting to be rescued. As Fran Norris Scoble notes in "In Search of the Female Hero": "We realized a . . . disturbing fact: that even in books which feature female characters, those characters are often what another ninth grade girl described as 'the worst women,' meaning, of course, they were women who she could neither admire nor identify with."*

The exclusion of women and girls as prominent players in such stories has reinforced their diminished role, but in today's changing world, there is a need for a new kind of hero who breaks free of the traditional restrictions of sex or age or race. Even though the stories of our culture lag behind, there are already plenty of real-life examples of female heroes for a new era.

Take the example of nine-year-old Anisa Kintz from South Carolina, who responded to racial tension in her community in South Carolina by organizing a conference called "Calling All Colors: A Race Unity Conference" that brought together more than two hundred people to discuss solutions to racism, particularly in the field of education. Media coverage of the conference eventually spread across the country and even internationally. Soon, the "Calling All Colors" initiative spread to other communities in South

---

* Fran Norris Scoble, "In Search of the Female Hero: Juliet Revisited," *English Journal*, vol. 75, no. 2 (Feb., 1986), p. 85.

Carolina. Kintz was recognized by the president of the United States as a "Point of Light" and the conferences still continue today.

Another girl, a ten-year-old named Samantha Smith, moved the world when she wrote to Yuri Andropov, then Soviet Communist Party general secretary, in 1982. Her heartfelt letter expressed her worries that the United States and the Soviet Union might get into a nuclear war and conveyed her belief that the two nations should live together in peace. Her letter became a stepping stone to better relations and peace. It catapulted Samantha to a position as an international ambassador for peace, increasing possibilities for cooperation between the two nations.

Despite the examples of Anisa Kintz, Samantha Smith, and many others who have broken traditional barriers and become heroes, many people still do not see girls and women as potential heroes. The need for stories that portray such heroes is clear.

The stories in this book provide positive examples of girls and women who learn to see their own capacity to create change. By embodying the heroic female spirit, these heroes serve not only to reflect a changing world, but also to help shape it.

The stories are inspired by the teachings of the Bahá'í Faith and reinforce the spiritual qualities that are important for the unity and progress of the whole human race, such as peacefulness, generosity, love, and recognizing the equality of all people.

Creating female heroes who exemplify these values also requires that the classical image of hero be reexamined—

the prototypical hero has long been defined as a powerful warrior, knight, king, or other male figure who fulfills some quest and performs feats of strength and courage, using power and force to subdue his enemies in the process. Usually these heroes, upon fulfilling their quests, are rewarded materially with riches and wealth and, of course, the hand of a beautiful woman in marriage.

But what does the *new* hero look like?

Heroic females try with all their might to reshape the world. They celebrate a freedom to choose, to raise their voices, to respond. This freedom is a wonderful, sometimes scary freedom that makes it possible for them to bring about change, to make a difference, and to embrace their own heroic spirit.

For a woman or girl to embody the heroic female spirit requires first spiritually and mentally accepting the possibility that she is destined to be a hero. She must recognize her equality with others and her self-worth.

Second, she must be willing to be detached from things of the world in pursuit of a higher self. She is a conqueror of self, willing to see the presence of God in both humanity and nature, and willing to use individual initiative and her own authority to help establish justice and peace in the world. The Bahá'í writings describe such detachment as essential to victory: "Our greatest efforts must be directed towards detachment from the things of the world; we must strive to become more spiritual, more luminous, to follow the counsel of the Divine Teaching, to serve the cause of unity and true equality, to be merciful, to reflect the love of the Highest on all men, so that the light of the Spirit shall be apparent in all our deeds, to the end that all humanity shall be united, the stormy sea thereof calmed, and all rough waves disappear from off the surface of life's ocean henceforth unruffled and peaceful."*

The next step after detachment is a willingness to make personal sacrifices for the sake of some higher aim. The heroic female is committed to being a living sacrifice, filled with the spirit of mercy, ready to receive spiritual gifts, and ready to experience the true joy that helps her recognize that she is serving and sacrificing for the glory of God, rather than being self-serving.

The heroes in this collection of stories are not only a departure from old models, they also face issues relevant to the world today such as war, prejudice, and environmental protection. The stories provide positive examples of characters who are actively engaged in improving the world around them. Each story is supplemented by commentary and discussion questions that will help readers to examine the underlying issues, attitudes, and thought processes that created the problems as well as the solutions in the story.

The first story, "The Legend of the Guardians of the Forest," illustrates the principle of interdependence, showing that every living thing in the world is connected and intermingled with every other thing and every person on earth. The story and the accompanying discussion questions emphasize the idea that everyone is responsible for the care of the earth and for preserving all of its resources.

---

* 'Abdu'l-Bahá, *Selections from the Writings of 'Abdu'l-Bahá* (Wilmette, IL: Bahá'í Publishing Trust, 1997), no. 28.19.

Other stories emphasize the importance of developing a unique identity. The character in "The Cave of Whispers" is trapped and can only escape by asserting her individuality, while "The Keeper of the Shoes" shows a girl who tries many different identities in her search for herself.

Some of these heroes must find creative solutions to their problems, like the princess in "The Princess and the Troublesome Dragon," who defeats a dragon without violence. In "The Girl Who Could Open Doors with Her Heart" it is pure intentions and willingness to do good that bring victory.

"The Girl Who Climbed a Ladder to the Stars" demonstrates the stifling effects of prejudice and shows a girl whose bravery teaches the world a lesson about establishing peace. Another girl teaches her village a lesson in "The Wall of Sorrows," this time by showing the value of acts of kindness.

The story "The Quest on the Holy Mountain" depicts the path we all must take towards unity, and the pitfalls we must overcome in our prejudices in order to discover it. "The Light of Unity" also shows the need for unity, and the need to sacrifice blaming others and instead learn forgiveness and kindness.

These stories clearly illustrate that the solutions to problems lie not in conflict and contention but in the quest for unity, which often requires having the courage to express new ideas and attempt novel solutions.

As Joseph Campbell wrote, "The hero-deed to be wrought is not today what it was in the century of Galileo. When then there was darkness, now there is light; but also, where light was there is now darkness. The modern hero-deed must be that of questing to bring to light again the lost Atlantis of the coordinated soul."*

The "coordinated soul" Campbell refers to can be seen as a unified human race, where people are valued for their contributions to the progress of humanity rather than because they are of a particular color, creed, or sex. The writings of the Bahá'í Faith emphasize that unity among people is a vital part of humanity's responsibility to promote an "ever-advancing civilization." As Bahá'u'lláh, the founder of the Bahá'í Faith, wrote: "The well-being of mankind, its peace and security, are unattainable unless and until its unity is firmly established."†

Not only will these stories inspire hope for this kind of world, they will show that women and girls can have a powerful and heroic role in creating it.

---

* Joseph Campbell, *The Hero with a Thousand Faces* (London: Fontana Press, 1993), p. 388.
† Bahá'u'lláh, *Gleanings from the Writings of Bahá'u'lláh* (Wilmette, IL: Bahá'í Publishing, 2005), no. 131.2.

Part I

A Collection of Tales

1

The Legend
of the Guardians
of the Forest

*O*nce upon a time not so long ago, there was a young girl named Terrah. She awakened early one morning just before dawn, suddenly aware of the fragrance of the wind gently blowing through her window. The soft aromas of the meadow and the forest beyond it flowed across her body and compelled her to sit up.

"What do you want? Leave me be!" she said.

"Come, come to the forest. The Great Tree is waiting for you," whispered the wind as it caressed her shoulders and played with her hair. The girl sleepily sat up, rubbed her eyes, and dangled her feet from the side of her bed.

"But I'm not allowed to go to the forest alone. Besides, it's dark in there, and the sun isn't up yet," she responded.

"Come, the Great Tree is waiting for you," answered the wind. "You will be able to find the path. The Great Tree will light the way."

The girl stood up and dressed herself. She looked out the window at the ancient forest that lay across the meadow. Yes, there was light coming from the center of the forest. She and many others had long wondered about the light that radiated from the midst of the towering trees, but no one had ever ventured forth to investigate what it came from. Now, perhaps, she would discover its source.

She left the hut and ventured into the familiar meadow. How would she find her way in the dark? It was not quite dawn yet. She knew of no path, and the brush was too thick for her to get through it. She quickened her pace in the moonlit meadow and soon approached the edge of the forest. "If it's too dark to find a pathway I'll have to turn back," she thought. Yet no sooner had the thought entered her mind than the trees began to bend their branches out of her way and form the path she was to follow.

The light emanating from the center of the forest seemed to grow brighter as she followed the path. As she drew closer to it, she began to feel deep awe and respect for the humble trees.

"Hurry," whispered the wind as it pushed her along the path and blew her hair across her face.

"I'm walking as fast as I can," she said. "Stop pushing me, please!" The girl heard the wind impatiently ruffling the leaves of the trees around her.

As she approached the Great Tree, her eyes widened and her jaw dropped. There it stood in all of its magnificence, tall and dignified, its great branches reaching out towards her. Brilliant light radiated from every branch, for each was covered with thousands upon thousands of butterflies. The butterflies' iridescent wings turned and quivered on every branch and twig, and the tree itself looked as if it might take flight at any moment, but of course it was firmly rooted in the ground. The girl looked at the trunk of the majestic tree and saw what appeared to be two large, sad eyes looking out at her.

"Why do you look so sad, Great Tree?" she asked.

"You must save us," whispered the tree.

"Save you?" the girl asked. "Are you in danger?"

"Yes, we are," replied the tree. "The people of the village plan to cut down this ancient forest. They must not do that, for there is a great treasure here." The Great Tree closed its eyes and sighed. The butterflies quivered in response.

"But why? What is this great treasure I must save?" asked the girl.

"The trees of the ancient forests are the lungs of this earth. They purify the air that all creatures must breathe. If the people of the village chop us down, the air will become thick and poisonous. They must turn back," said the tree. "If they chop us down, terrible things will happen. When the rains come, our roots will no longer be able to hold the soil and it will be washed away, along with all of the villagers' crops. Without crops, the villagers' cattle will die, for they will have nothing to eat. Without crops or cattle, what will the people eat? Tell the people they must turn back. There are also thousands of plants in the forest that could be used as medicine to heal many diseases if only the people would take the time to study and investigate. Tell them to turn back! This community of trees is very important to the entire world!" said the Great Tree.

"Oh, how terrible!" said Terrah. "I must save you. I must save us all! I will tell the villagers. I am sure they will listen.

I know they will. And I will tell all the farmers and the woodsmen. Surely they will understand."

"Hopefully you can convince them. But if not, I will send the forest to aid you," the Great Tree told her. "The spirit of the forest will protect you."

As Terrah ran through the towering trees of the forest, they bent their branches to form a pathway for her. Twice she stumbled and almost fell, but the branches of the nearby trees reached out to support her and prevent the fall. The wind assisted the girl as she ran, and soon she found herself nearing the edge of the forest, approaching the meadow.

Terrah saw the people of the village in the distance. She could see they were all carrying something with them. They were coming with shovels! They carried rakes, and hoes, and hatchets. Some pulled carts behind them, and others carried tinderboxes in their hands. Seeing this, Terrah ran with abandon, tears flowing down her cheeks, feeling as if her heart would burst. She startled the villagers when she suddenly appeared and met them at the edge of the forest.

"Stop!" she cried. "I know your plans. You intend to chop down this ancient forest, but you must not do that!"

"And why not?" the people of the village demanded. "We need wood to build new homes and keep them warm, and we must clear the land so we can farm it. We need this land, and the trees are merely taking up space. You are standing in the way of progress! Who do you think you are? You can't tell us what to do!"

"There is a great treasure within the ancient forest," Terrah said.

"What are you talking about?" the villagers asked, suddenly growing quiet. The people of the village became very attentive at the mention of treasure. They were very interested in all kinds of treasures, for treasures carried the promise of wealth and riches that would improve their standard of living. "What kind of treasure?" they inquired.

"The trees of the ancient forest are the lungs of the earth. They purify the air that we breathe. Without them, the air would become thick and poisonous. They provide us with the gift of fresh air; that is the treasure. They make it possible for us to breathe pure, clean air. You must turn back!" said the girl.

"What kind of nonsense is this?" the villagers said with scorn. "Trees don't have lungs. They can't breathe. They just sit there taking up space that could be put to better use. Get out of our way!" they ordered. "We're going to clear the land to plant crops and raise cattle. You can't stand in the way of progress, and you can't tell us what to do. Your ideas are ridiculous!"

"No, no!" Terrah begged. "Please listen! If you cut down the ancient forest, terrible things will happen. The roots of the trees will no longer be able to hold the soil when the rains come, and the water will wash away your crops. When the soil and your crops wash away, your cattle will starve, and then what will you do? You must turn back!"

"Get out of our way, you impudent girl! Wait until your parents hear what you've done today. You should be ashamed of yourself! You're an embarrassment to the whole village," they shouted. "You don't know what you're talking about. The village needs this land for planting more crops and grazing more cattle. You can't stand in the way of progress!"

Then someone in the crowd whose heart was very hard threw a rake at the girl. Its handle hit her on the shoulder, and she began to bleed. Someone else threw a shovel at her. Its handle hit her on the forehead, and blood ran down her face. She bent over and picked up the shovel and the rake. She stood fast and held them out in front of her, grasping the wooden handle of each and raising them up to the sky.

All at once the crowd heard a humming sound coming from the ancient forest. They looked beyond the girl and saw what appeared to be a great black cloud rising above the forest behind her. It was filled with hundreds of thousands of birds and grasshoppers, toads and frogs, and all manner of creatures of the forest. The cloud of creatures hummed and twisted across the great expanse of the meadow until it reached and surrounded the girl. As it hovered above and around her, in one voice it hummed, "We are a community. We are not a commodity to be used and discarded. Turn back. Turn back!"

The people of the village murmured and grumbled. They found the cloud of animals and insects strange and frightening, but they weren't ready to back down to a swarm of birds and insects and other inferior creatures. "We're taking the land for our crops. We need the wood to build furniture and houses. We need to raise more cattle. It's a necessity! Get out of our way now!" they shouted.

A villager picked up a rock and threw it at Terrah, and then someone else threw another. Soon all of the villagers were throwing rocks. They stoned the girl.

She stood there, making no attempt to escape, and the blood flowed down her arms. When the red blood touched the brown wood of the handles of the rake and the shovel, a very strange thing began to happen. The wood began to turn green. Roots began to sprout and reach into the ground, and green branches and leaves sprouted from the handles. The branches began to grow around the girl's body, and soon she was encased in a trunk that both protected and supported her now almost lifeless, barely conscious body.

Slowly the people of the village approached the tree. They could see the girl's eyes peering out at them from inside the trunk. Then a strange thing happened. All the butterflies that had been perched on the branches of the Great Tree now left the Great Tree in one mass and flew to the tree in which the girl was encased. As they descended, a great, white light surrounded her, giving her hope of transformation as she realized all was not lost.

The people gasped and drew back in surprise. "What have we done?" asked one villager.

"How can we tell her kin?" asked another.

The people turned back and retreated to the village. When they arrived, they called to Terrah's parents in their hut.

"What is it?" her parents asked.

"We have done a terrible thing to your daughter, and we do not know how to undo it. We are ashamed of ourselves. We have harmed Terrah, and she has turned into a tree. Come to the meadow," they said.

Terrah's parents ran to the meadow and soon learned what had happened. They were filled with grief when they saw their daughter's eyes sadly peering out at them from the trunk of the tree. In their grief and distress they hugged the tree, and at once the girl within the tree began to cry. Great tears ran down the trunk of the tree, and because they were tears of compassion and forgiveness, they seared a long narrow opening down the length of the tree. Terrah's parents could see their daughter's body trapped inside the tree. In their desperation to help their daughter, they began to pull and tear at the trunk with their hands and soon pried it open.

Eventually Terrah stepped out, whole and healthy, but something about her was different. Something new had been added to her body. She now had a brilliant pair of iridescent, butterfly-like wings. Slowly she opened them, and as she did so the people of the village saw how truly humble and generous she was. They bowed their heads before her grace, and she smiled at them.

Then, from deep within the forest, the people heard a horrible, painful wailing sound. It seemed to be coming from the center of the ancient forest. It was as if something were dying in terrible anguish.

Now Terrah had received great powers through her transformation and she felt intuitively that every single thing in the universe was connected; the villagers who in their need had sought to destroy the forest, the animals and plants, the Great Tree itself. Tears of compassion ran down her cheeks.

Terrah knew that it was not a person or an animal that made the sound—she felt that it must be that the Great Tree was dying. She shook her wings and then leaped into the sky, beseeching the people of the village to follow her through the forest. They watched in awe as the trees humbly bent their branches to form a path for them to pass through to the Great Tree.

Soon all were gathered before the Great Tree. They found that all of the tree's leaves had fallen to the ground except one last living leaf, which dangled from a branch way up high. But now that the Great Tree saw the transformation in Terrah and the people of the village, he drew increasing strength from them. He also felt enveloped by compassion. The girl gently embraced the tree. The tree was so grateful that it began to weep, and as it wept, great tears of forgiveness flowed down the length of its trunk. Terrah was amazed to see that the tears seared a narrow opening through the trunk. She could see a boy's body trapped inside the trunk. She called for help, and soon all the people of the village were engaged in trying to release the boy.

Several of the villagers began to tug on the edges of the opening in the tree until finally it peeled back and the young boy stepped out. Like Terrah, he emerged from the trunk with great iridescent butterfly-like wings of radiant colors. He began to speak.

"I have been trapped inside this tree for one hundred years, for that is how long ago I tried to save the ancient forest from our ancestors. In order to save the forest from destruction, I became a part of this ancient tree, which gave me power over the forest-dwellers. My powers allowed me to create a fortress out of the brambles, bushes, and trees in order to protect the ancient forest. Then I was able to fend off the attackers who would harm the forest by using the animals and other forest resources. But when the misguided villagers of the past grew greater in numbers, I realized that my powers were not sufficient. So I sent the wind in search of a receptive heart to help me. My anger and bitterness at the villagers actually blocked my ability to forgive. But seeing all of you come here to save me, something changed. My forgiveness has now released me. Thank you for rescuing me, Terrah, and thank you for saving this ancient forest. The lesson I have learned is that no one can guard the ancient forest alone. It must be done in a spirit of cooperation, with everyone united in thought."

The girl grasped the boy's hand and smiled at him.

The people of the village gathered in a group and began discussing very loudly and earnestly how they were going to resolve their need for wood. Some said, "We should have chopped down the forest anyway," but others quickly silenced them. After they came to an agreement, the leader of the village approached the girl and the boy. He said, "You have taught us the meaning and importance of a noble sacrifice. We understand that there's an important balance in nature that mustn't be upset. We have decided to work to maintain the balance instead of trying to use it for short-term gains. We've decided to plant more trees every year. We'll sacrifice our desire for wealth to protect this vital community of animals, insects, plants, and trees, just as you have sacrificed and shown us the way. Thank goodness we didn't destroy both you and the forest!"

The boy was going to speak, but then it occurred to him that his new friend, Terrah, might have something to say, so he held his peace. Sure enough, she came before the group. She smiled kindly at all of the villagers and said,

"Every little ant, every fish, every creature, every blade of grass, every living thing, every drop of water, every rock and stone, and every inch of air on this planet has purpose. They are all interconnected and must be cherished and protected. Live in peace and with respect and we will share all of our gifts with you for all of eternity."

A spokesperson for the villagers came forth to offer a heartfelt response: "We are thankful to witness this incredible transformation of our own thoughts and understanding and beg of you to become the guardians of this forest. We hope you will teach us more about how to be kind to the earth."

Terrah and her newfound friend turned and looked into one another's eyes, smiling in silent agreement. From that day forward, they lived together as guardians of the forest, protecting it from destruction and educating the people of the village about the world of nature. And thus began the legend of the Guardians of the Forest.

2

The Cave
of Whispers

*T*here once was a young woman named Nedonis who lived in a cave. Those who have never lived in a cave might think it strange for a young woman to live in such a dark place, but she didn't find it so. She had lived there for all of her fifteen years and had grown accustomed to it, for it was all she had ever known. But she did enjoy peering out of the cave to watch what was going on in the world outside.

The young woman often held her hand to her chest as she looked at the world outside, as if what she were seeing were almost more than she could bear. What she saw was breathtaking, for the world beyond the cave was filled with sunshine, colorful flowers, and busy people walking to and fro. Children were laughing and playing games. Sometimes strange and beautiful music wafted through the air. It was a lot to take in. As the young woman watched and listened, sometimes you could see a wistful look in her eyes. At times, if you looked very closely, you might even see a hint of tears. Nedonis didn't understand the tears and couldn't explain them if you asked what they were for, but they seemed to come whenever she spent a great deal of time gazing at what was beyond the cave.

When that happened, to avoid being seen, Nedonis would turn away from the sunshine and the world outside and head back into the comfortable, familiar darkness of the cave, the only home she had known since her parents had died. There were many rooms in the cave. Those that were in the deepest recesses of the cave were so dark that she had to feel her way around as she walked through them, but she had become very good at this over the years. In fact, she was an expert at navigating her way around the cave in the dark.

People would occasionally gather around the entrance to the cave and ask Nedonis to come out and join in what they were doing. As much as Nedonis longed to join them, she could only smile shyly and draw back. They all looked so bright and happy and pretty. She knew that she wasn't like them and worried that if she even stepped into the sunlight where they could see her better, they would run away. She felt ashamed and turned back to the cave as a mysterious whisper on the wind curled through all the rooms of the cave and drew her away from the other children.

She couldn't see the origin of the sounds, which were quiet but maddeningly persistent. They emerged mysteriously from the depths of the cave and filled her with the sense that no matter what might be in there, going beyond the cave was a dangerous idea. Somehow the sounds seemed distant and yet impossibly close, seeping into her.

A whisper curled around the young woman's arms and legs. She was hardly aware of it at all, and yet she knew it was there. Whenever she looked beyond the cave into the world outside, almost effortlessly, but firmly, the whisper discouraged her from approaching the mouth of the cave too closely or, heaven forbid, going beyond it into the world outside.

How can a wispy, insubstantial thing such as a whisper hold a young woman so firmly? What power does a whisper have? Nedonis had never questioned the whisper. She had merely allowed it to discourage her, and in this way it had restrained her.

There was a wise old woman, Sophia, a healer who lived in the village, not far from the cave. She had often passed by the entrance to the cave and had witnessed the young woman's furtive glances at the outside world. She had seen the longing in the young woman's eyes when the sun penetrated the darkness of the cave. When dusk fell, the wise old woman could hear the whisper as it echoed from the walls of the cave. She shivered in her bed as she listened. It was a sound that struck at the core of every good thing she believed in. She said a prayer to the Great One. "O Great One! Give this young woman your power to defeat this ever-present, insidious foe."

The woman fell into a deep sleep and her dreams were penetrated by fragments of ancient memories. She saw images of a girl moving at the mouth of the cave, smiling and gathering wildflowers when dark whispers emerged and snagged her ankles. In the dream vision, the whispers looked like sinister clouds, covered in jabbering mouths. Though the girl tried to run, the mouths convinced her it would do no good. She couldn't see that the clouds, though cold and sharp against her skin, had no substance. Instead of running away, she was in a daze. The whispers beckoned her into the cave and silently, with shoulders down, she went. Her family searched, but the whispers reached their ears, too, and confused their minds and made them ignore the cave. They wandered away, cursed to forget her.

The old woman awoke to a storm the next morning well before dawn, disturbed by her dream. She knew that the dream had shown her a vision of a curse that afflicted Nedonis.

The old woman stood up and looked out the window at the storm. Lightning filled the sky, and thunder rolled over the hills to the west. When the lightning flashed, every branch and twig of the tree outside her window was outlined in silver. And when it flashed again, the tree shook violently as a luminescent finger of lightening touched the highest branch. Out shot the lightning, straight from the lowest branch that all the neighborhood children had climbed and played upon. The branch glowed as if it were fire-hot, but it did not burst into flame.

The old woman opened the door to her hut and approached the tree. She reached out to touch the branch but quickly withdrew her hand when her movement brought a clap of thunder. She said another prayer to the Great One: "O Great One! Show me your wish for the girl in the cave. She is too dear to remain in the darkness."

The branch trembled violently until a leafless stick about four feet long fell from the tree. The old woman picked up the stick, and as she did so, a clap of thunder rolled through the village. She waved the stick at the sky and another clap of thunder roared. She laughed and danced a joyous dance at this wondrous sign from the heavens. She knew what she must do now!

Sophia smiled knowingly as she walked in the dark towards the cave. Lightning flashed across the sky, and shadows fluttered on her path. When she arrived at the mouth of the cave, she placed the thunder-stick in a spot where the young woman would be certain to see it at sunrise. A confident smile played across the old woman's lips as she returned to her home.

At dawn the young woman awoke, stretching her long arms to the ceiling of the cave and extending her toes toward the entrance. She sensed that something was different but could not name it. What had changed? She looked around the cave. Sunlight was streaming in from the morning sun at the mouth of the cave, while the ever-present whispers were curling around each ray of light as if to choke it. Nothing looked any different.

Nedonis looked at the ground immediately outside the mouth of the cave, and there it lay, shining in the sunlight— a long stick. "How convenient! I can use that stick to stoke my fire tonight," said the young woman, reaching out to pick it up. It would be perfect for the task. Yet the moment she touched the stick there was a great and mysterious clap of thunder!

She was startled and frightened by the sound, but intrigued. As she drew closer, she saw that what she had thought were reflections from the sun actually emerged from the stick itself. What looked like tiny arcs of lightning moved across the surface of the wood. Instead of stoking her fire, she thought, this stick would mean that she would need no more fire. The wind and whispers in the cave had always extinguished torches, but perhaps the light from this talisman would enable her to finally reach the depths of the cave and see the source of the whispers that kept her captive.

She touched the stick again. Again there was a clap of thunder, but no harm was done. She picked up the stick and held it.

The whispers swirled into the room and began to encircle the young woman. She stopped to listen with curiosity. What were the whispers saying? She tried to decipher what she heard, but the whispers raced by too quickly for her to make sense of them. Although she couldn't make out any words, the whispers left her with an ominous feeling that darkened and grew stronger. Indeed, the whispers seemed to pierce her very skin and penetrate her heart.

Nedonis dropped the stick as she felt the whispers curling tightly around her wrist. It was as if the whispers were trying to prevent her from keeping the thunder-stick. Quickly reaching down with her other hand, she grabbed the stick again and ran into another room trying to escape the whispers. She clung to the stick. It thundered and rumbled, reverberating against the walls of the cave, and the flickering light from it shed a bluish glow that lit the cave walls.

What was that?

There! She listened carefully and heard it again. The whispers surrounded her but seemed unable to reach her while she held the thunder-stick.

"Don't think!" the whispers said, moving at the edges of the light.

How could that be? How very strange! Surely the whispers had not said that. She had never recognized any meaning in the whispers before, but it had been very distinct. There was no mistaking what she had heard. Why would the whispers say such a thing to her? Weren't they there to protect her, to keep her safe from harm?

The whispers continued. They said, "Be quiet!"

The young woman's mouth suddenly began to feel paralyzed.

The whispers said, "Pay no attention to what's going on out there!"

The young woman began to feel numb, as if she were in a trance.

The whispers said, "Don't get too close to anyone!" and she almost withdrew from her own soul.

"You don't need anything!" they said, and she began to feel listless and apathetic. Her grip on the thunder-stick loosened. As the light dimmed and the thunder quieted, the whispers came closer, trying to reach her.

But while the young woman was holding the stick, she began to think about what the whispers were saying. Perhaps the whispers were right, and maybe they were protecting her from the world outside. . . . But she couldn't help wondering, "What if they are wrong?"

She reaffirmed her grip on the thunder-stick and swung it wildly in the air. Shimmering light danced upon her hand, and a crash of thunder scattered the whispers. She ran into an adjoining room to escape the whispers, but they rose up to follow her.

"You can't go out there!" they said. "It's dangerous!" "You don't want to be different!" they said. "Stay here! We will take care of you and keep you safe." "You are weak!" the whispers said. "You won't be able to manage out there. You aren't pretty enough. Look at how plain your clothes are! You won't know what to do or who to trust! Stay here! You need us!"

Nedonis raised the thunder-stick once more and pummeled the wraith-like whispers that swirled around her in the dark. They whirled around the young woman's neck as if to strangle her with phantom tendrils. They would have, too, had not a blast from the thunder-stick exploded, forcing the whispers to retreat and creep stealthily along the rock walls, waiting for yet another opportunity to attack.

The young woman whirled around as the whispers trailed at her heels, circling her toes, trying to trip her. She almost lost her footing but nimbly leapt aside, practically falling into the next room. Holding the thunder-stick high above her head, she shook it in a frenzy while the cunning whispers said, "You don't need to go out there to be happy!" "You don't need to feel the sunshine. Stay in here where it's dark, and safe, and familiar!" "Don't try new things. That's foolish and dangerous!" "You don't know yourself. We know what you need. You need us!" "Stop!"

The thunder-stick boomed and rattled, illuminating the cave, exposing every evil whisper to its brilliant light, forcing all of the dark whispers away from the young woman.

By now the young woman was shaking uncontrollably and the thunder-stick was pulling her toward the entrance of the cave. She was terrified. If she didn't release the thunder-stick, it was going to drag her right through the opening into the world outside. She was frantically pulling in the opposite direction while the whispers made a last-ditch effort to snatch the thunder-stick from her hand, saying, "You're not capable of making these choices!" "Don't ask questions!" "Don't change!" "Don't challenge us!"

With a zealous, snake-like rattle, the thunder-stick scattered every remnant of the evil whispers and threw the young woman outside, into the sunlight.

Nedonis lay there, frightened and spent, the thunder-stick still in her hand. All the villagers crowded around her, amazed to see her, tangled black hair falling in her face, blinking in the bright light of day. They all began to chatter at once. Alarmed, she nervously began to swing the thunder-stick in a wide circle around her. The crowd jumped back as the stick thundered loudly. The wise old woman made her way to the front of the crowd.

"Nedonis, all the evil whispers are gone now. You are safe. There's no need to shake the thunder-stick again!" she said.

"But I'm afraid these people are going to make me go back inside the cave, and I don't want to do that," said the young woman.

"If they do, all you have to do is say 'No!' very firmly," said the old woman reassuringly. And so Nedonis did. She practiced saying, "No!" for quite a while.

She now knew that the whispers that she had thought were comforting were actually harming her. She looked at the thunder-stick, then she touched the end of it to her head as if to awaken herself. At that moment, she began to have new thoughts she had never had before. "Look forward to change. Ask questions. Challenge every whisper. Stay in the sunshine where you'll be happy. You need these wonderful, welcoming people in the village."

Soon the whispers left her entirely, and she ventured back to the cave to be sure that the whispers were truly gone. Sophia agreed to accompany her, and together they approached the cave. Though Nedonis was nervous, she held the thunder-stick tightly and entered, knowing that she understood now how to protect herself. Together she and Sophia made their way through the cave. No trace of the whispers remained. The only sounds in the caverns were their own voices and the echo of the thunder-stick. And with the light from the thunder-stick, Nedonis saw for the first time how cramped and dirty the cave was and wondered how she had lived there for so long.

Nedonis's eyes adjusted to the light of the sun, and her pale skin warmed from the sunlight. She was finally free, but she would not forget her time in the cave. She took a place in the village as Sophia's assistant and was free not only to create and to heal, but to help others heal as well.

3

The Keeper of the Shoes

*O*nce there was a nine-year-old girl named Raven who sometimes found it difficult to be herself. Her mother and father loved her as much as all good parents love their children, and most of the time she felt that all was well with the world. For the most part it was. But there were also times when Raven thought, "I wish I liked myself. It's so hard to be me. Sometimes I'm so quiet nobody knows I'm around, and other times my parents say I'm so boisterous that nobody can ignore me. How am I supposed to act? Why don't more people like me, and why don't they notice me the way I want them to?"

One snowy winter day Raven's parents announced that they were going to be holding a dinner party to which all of their friends were invited. Raven was given the responsibility to answer the door and take the guests' coats when they arrived. Raven stood at the door, looking out the window, deep in thought as she watched the snowflakes fall and waited for the guests to begin arriving. She felt rather small, and the world seemed so big.

There were so many different people in the world, and it seemed as if half the world were going to be arriving at their home for the party that night. She was going to greet many wonderful, intelligent, interesting, and diverse people. Her parents had invited a lot of important people who did important things, and she was a little nervous about greeting them. Maybe she was a little shy. But before she had time to dwell on that thought, the doorbell rang.

Raven opened the door. "Hello!" she said a little timidly.

"Hello!" said Mr. Tinker, who worked as a professional clown. He was stopping by the party after a gig at a local family restaurant where he had been making balloon animals and entertaining kids who got bored while their parents were eating. Although he had apparently had time to remove his face makeup, he was still wearing his clown suit and big shoes.

"Good evening, Mr. Tinker. Please come in," she said, smiling and feeling more comfortable.

"Thank you, Raven. How are you this evening?" He took off his coat and handed it to Raven, who began to hang it up. "May I leave my shoes here?" he asked.

"Why do you want to take your shoes off?" Raven responded.

"Well," he said, "it's snowing outside, and I don't imagine your parents would want me to track snow into your house. Besides, nobody wants to be a clown all the time. I could use a break this evening."

"Sure, Mr. Tinker, you can leave your shoes right there. I'll keep an eye on them. Have a nice time at the party," she said.

Soon the doorbell rang again.

Raven opened the door.

"Good evening. May I come in?" asked Dr. Farid, who was a surgeon.

"Of course, Dr. Farid, come right in," said Raven. "May I take your coat?" The doctor gave her his coat. "May I put my shoes over here?" he asked, pointing to Mr. Tinker's clown shoes.

"Why do you want to take off your shoes?" Raven asked.

"Well, you have such a clean white carpet, and I don't want to get it dirty." He leaned closer and whispered, "To tell the truth, as long as I'm wearing these shoes, I feel like I'm still at work. It's been a very long day at the hospital, and I've been on my feet since early this morning. I just feel like relaxing tonight." He put his shoes next to the clown shoes and headed into the living room to join the party.

The doorbell rang again.

Raven peered out the window in the door. It was Dr. Starkweather, who was a professor of English literature. She quickly opened the door to let her in.

"Hello, Dr. Starkweather," she said. "Please come in. May I take your coat?"

"Why thank you, Raven," said the professor, removing her coat and handing it to the girl. "Shall I take my shoes off and leave them here?"

"Sure," said Raven. "I'll keep an eye on them."

"Oh, thank you," said the professor. "I'm glad to get out of them. It seems as if all I do all day long is stand on my feet and talk about Shakespeare. I get so tired, and sometimes I have the feeling I may as well be talking to myself because none of my students has read the assignments anyway. It will feel so good to get off my feet and not have to worry about leading any discussions." She took off her shoes and headed for the living room.

Once again the doorbell rang.

Raven opened the door a crack to see who was there. There stood Mrs. Earnest, the mayor, wrapped in a beautiful fox coat and wearing an elegant pair of shoes. Raven quickly opened the door all the way so as not to appear rude. "Hello, Mayor Earnest! Would you like to come in?"

"Yes, thank you, I would," answered the mayor. She strode in and removed her coat and handed it to Raven. "I've been on my feet in these shoes all afternoon, meeting the public. It will be good to get out of them. Shall I leave them over there?" she asked.

"Yes, yes, of course," said Raven. She thought for a moment and looked at the mayor inquisitively. "Is it very hard to be the mayor?" she asked.

"Oh yes, my dear! Very hard," the mayor responded. "You have to be strong and sensible all the time, ready to deal with the city's problems, whatever they may be, no matter when they arise, day or night. You have to collect your wits to face the public nearly every day of the year and act perfectly dignified, even when you're sick, or tired, or you simply don't feel like it. And no matter where you go, nearly everyone knows who you are, so you don't have any privacy. Everyone wants to talk to you, but they never want to listen. But now that I've got my shoes off—"

Before the mayor could finish her sentence, the doorbell rang again. More guests were arriving.

"Well, you weren't asking to hear the story of my life, were you?" the mayor said then headed down the hall to join the party.

Raven opened the door, and there before her stood Mr. Lawson, who was a lawyer. "Hello, Mr. Lawson. How are you?"

He answered, "I'm fine, but if I have to walk one more step in these shoes tonight—"

"Oh, please come in and take them off so you can relax, and I'll bet you'll have a wonderful time at the party," said Raven.

Mr. Lawson came in and took off his shoes, adding them to the growing pile, then took off his coat and gave it to Raven, saying, "Thank you, my dear. Bless you!" He made his way down the hall to join the rest of the party.

Raven pulled the door open not knowing what or whom to expect, so many people had already arrived. It was Ms. Monica Morall, who was a social worker. She was known for getting into heavy moral and philosophical discussions when she was with friends. She got right to the point. "I've been deep in thought, listening for many hours, trying to help people solve their personal problems all day long. May I take my shoes off and leave them in this pile by the door? I'm ready to kick back and have some fun tonight."

"Yes, please do!" replied the girl. And there certainly was a pile of shoes by now.

The doorbell rang yet again. "Excuse me while I greet our next guest," said Raven.

Raven opened the door and was surprised to see Mr. Carver, a local artist who was known for his unusual sculptures and his eccentric ways. His unusual clothes and eyeglasses gave the impression of an offbeat, creative genius, and Raven admired his unique style.

Mr. Carver took off his overcoat and shoes, sighed a deep sigh, and said, "I'm so glad to be here tonight! I'm going to just coast for a while, sit in a quiet corner, and listen to others. I'm so glad I don't have to attend yet another gallery opening and talk about my work right now." He walked into the living room where the rest of the people were gathered.

Raven stood near the pile of shoes, waiting for the doorbell to ring again, but it didn't. Apparently everyone who was coming to the party had arrived. She looked at the pile of shoes before her. Each pair seemed as different as the person who wore it, and yet each of them fascinated her.

She glanced in at the party, admiring each of the guests. They were all doing their best to help people in a way that suited their talents. And yet they were clearly all exhausted, so none of them had an easy time of it. Raven wondered if she would be a doctor, a mayor, or a clown. "Is there a best choice?" she wondered. Maybe she could find out by slipping into the shoes herself.

She looked at Mr. Tinker's clown shoes. It would be fun to try them out.

She pulled the clown shoes out from the pile and put them on her feet. They were huge and floppy, which made it very awkward to walk in them, and this made her laugh. She ran through the living room with the gigantic floppy clown shoes, and everyone laughed at her. For a few minutes she felt very clever and funny clowning around in the shoes, but this activity quickly lost its novelty, and the adults soon went back to their conversations. She began to feel rather silly. She could see that it was hard work to make everyone laugh. It took an awful lot of energy to keep everyone laughing. That was enough of that.

She went back to the front door and gazed at the pile of shoes. She took off the clown shoes and put on the doctor's shoes, then walked back to the living room to try them out. Almost as soon as she entered the room, the guests began turning to her to tell her how they were feeling and to ask her advice for all their little aches and pains and ailments. She found this quite strange; it was as if they thought she herself were the doctor! The mayor admitted to having a slight cough and wondered what to take for it. Should she take an expectorant? A decongestant? Would an over-the-counter preparation be advisable, or would something else be better? Professor Starkweather had fallen on the ice and bruised her hip. Could Raven recommend a pain reliever? Should she treat the injury with ice, or was it too late for that? Dr. Farid wanted Raven to examine his bunion, which had been bothering him for some time and was making it hard for him to maintain his daily exercise routine. What could she recommend for his bunion? Raven scurried out of the living room and back to the front door and the pile of shoes. Why was everybody speaking to her as if *she* were the doctor? No wonder the doctor didn't want to wear his shoes at the party! She quickly flung the shoes off her feet and put them back in the pile. She pondered which pair to try next.

She settled on Professor Starkweather's shoes, which were stylish but sturdy and serious looking. When she put them on, she suddenly began to feel very smart. She walked through the party in them and—miraculously—found herself able to recite Milton and Shakespeare to anyone who would listen. Mr. Carver, the artist, thought her very intelligent and listened intently and quietly. Raven was amazed at her sudden knowledge of poetry and literature, but she didn't feel comfortable reciting it in front of the guests at the party. It just didn't strike her as appropriate behavior for that gathering. So she ran back to the front door to change shoes again.

She put the professor's shoes back and slipped her feet into the mayor's shoes. They looked and felt very elegant, and she smiled to herself, thinking about what it would be like to be mayor. She walked back into the party. All eyes were on her, and she began to feel self-conscious. She felt a strong pressure to be perfectly dignified and to avoid making any kind of mistake whatsoever. This thought made her so anxious that she could hardly breathe. All around her the guests were saying, "Oh, look at Raven. How perfectly wise and wonderful she is!" Raven did not like this pressure to be perfect at all, so she ran back to the pile of shoes and took off the mayor's elegant shoes.

She spied Mr. Lawson's shoes, put them on, and went back into the crowded party room. Some guests looked at her with obvious admiration while others looked at her with contempt. While wearing the lawyer's shoes, she got the distinct feeling that he was a very generous, humble man who was proud of his work and very patient with people who were often unkind. She felt sad as she walked in his shoes and decided to take them off.

She returned them to the pile and exchanged them for Ms. Morall's shoes. When she went back into the party, her eyes met the lawyer's eyes, and she was struck with the thought that justice requires a champion and that champions of justice are not always appreciated. She thought on this a while. To do what was right was not always easy, and to do what was easy was definitely not always right.

She walked back to the pile of shoes and took off Ms. Morall's shoes so she could try on the last pair—Mr. Carver's comfortable shoes. When she put them on, she suddenly felt an overwhelming desire to create something beautiful and portray a great idea about the world as she saw it. How would she do this? It occurred to her that she might do it in many different ways, but maybe not all of them would be understood well by others. If she wasn't careful, her beautiful creation could be taken to mean something completely different than what she intended. She felt the delicious freedom of an artist's soul, but she saw that it was a freedom that needed discipline and wisdom, and she came to realize that all artists must be responsible.

At this point Raven realized she had tried on all the shoes. She felt as if she knew each of the guests at the party a little better now, and she had discovered that it wasn't easy to be anyone! She gathered up all the shoes, intending to put them back in order before the guests reclaimed them, but the party was already ending. One by one the guests were starting to depart, and they needed their shoes and coats. There would be no time for straightening up. She would just have to do her best to get the shoes back to their rightful owners.

The mayor was ready to leave first because she had to make sure she got to a press conference on time.

"Here are your shoes, Mayor Earnest," said Raven. In her haste to help the mayor, Raven inadvertently gave her a right shoe and a wrong shoe, for one was the clown's left shoe. In her hurry to be on her way to the press conference, the mayor put on her coat and slipped both shoes on, remarking, "Why, my left shoe doesn't hurt anymore! This has been a great party. I feel so relaxed—as if I could relax and maybe even be silly at the right time and in the right place and it wouldn't hurt a thing! Thank you so much for your hospitality. Good night!" Then she left.

Raven gave Mr. Tinker his other shoe and the mayor's right shoe. She wasn't quite sure how this was going to work out. What would a clown do with one clown shoe and an elegant woman's pump? But the mayor hadn't seemed to mind, so perhaps it was worth a try. Mr. Tinker put on the mismatched shoes and his coat and blithely left, feeling happy and exuding an air of quiet dignity and composure that he had never felt before. Realizing for the first time that he held the same goal as the mayor—seeking the common good for humanity.

Raven managed to give Mr. Lawson, the lawyer, one of his own shoes and one that belonged to Mr. Carver, the artist. That turned out to be a good combination because the soul of the lawyer yearned to express beauty even as he sought justice for others.

Raven exchanged one of the social worker's shoes with one of the doctor's shoes, and Ms. Morall walked out telling everyone to take good care of their health, because life has more meaning and purpose if one is healthy.

The doctor got one of his own shoes and one of Professor Starkweather's shoes, and he walked out saying he needed to find a couple of poetry books to take home to read. He thought maybe a little poetry and humor might help him improve his bedside manner and his doctor–patient relationships. Mr. Carver, the artist, put on his one shoe, and Raven slipped the lawyer's other shoe onto the other foot. He left the party with the thought that he would forevermore base his art on the principle of justice.

Professor Starkweather ended up with what was left: one of her own shoes and the last shoe, which really belonged to Ms. Morall, the social worker. She said as she left, "The pen is mightier than the sword, unless the sword is being wielded for the social good. But since both are symbols and enchantments abound, perhaps our two classes should debate the finer points of this conundrum."

Raven smiled as she closed the door behind the last guest and her parents began to clean up the glasses, plates, and dishes from the party. Wearing all of the other shoes had been exciting, but exhausting. She looked down at her own shoes, which were simple white sneakers.

She was happy that her parents had invited such a diverse group of people so she could see such different perspectives. Each of her parents' friends was like a flower in a garden. They all had different shapes, colors and fragrances, but each contributed to the beauty of the whole. She, too, was a flower, and she decided that she could be happy with herself after all—quiet and reserved at times, loud and boisterous at others—as long as she could find her place in the garden.

She saw now that she could choose her own shoes when she got older, and that they wouldn't have to be just one kind or another. She could choose one that was a clown's and one an artist's, or one that was a doctor's and one a philosopher's. She could become anything she really wanted to become as long as she was true to whatever gifts she discovered within herself and used them, as her guests did, to be of service to others.

4

The Girl
Who Could Open Doors
with Her Heart

*K*ing Shevon, like so many rulers before him, was unsatisfied with his rule. He desired complete obedience from his subjects and wished that the very sound of his voice would compel them to obey his wishes. He was not a cruel man, but he craved more power, unlike queen Raisa, who was wisely less controlling and more beneficent toward the people. Little did King Shevon know that the wind was listening to him and, hearing his desire to command, decided to carry his wishes far and wide, though not in the way that he hoped.

One night as he slept, worries that thieves would try to steal his royal treasures crept into his dreams. He awoke in the middle of the night in a panic. "Let no one open that door!" he called out, referring to the door to the royal treasury.

The next morning he rushed down to the treasury to make sure it was still secure, but when he tried to open the door to inspect his riches, he found that it was stuck fast. He called the captain of the guards—a huge brute of a man—who pushed and kicked, but the door remained stuck. He called the commander of the knights, an intelligent and resourceful man who had saved the kingdom numerous times, but after ten hearty heaves and ten hefty hos, he had dents in his armor, and still the door would not open.

Realizing that brute strength and sheer intelligence weren't enough, the king called the architect who had designed the castle, thinking surely he could find a way around the door. The man scratched his head, looked at the blueprints, and investigated the structure but could find no way in. Thinking perhaps it was a problem with the locks, the king summoned the royal locksmith. After trying key after key after key and hearing click after tumble after click with no results, the locksmith declared that it was not the lock.

Within days the king was running out of money. There were many things that needed to be done. He and the queen were planning a lavish holiday celebration and the date was fast approaching. There were plans to be made and food to be bought. There were dresses and suits to be tailored, and gifts to be purchased. He began to grow despondent.

In despair, the king sent for the wizard. When the wizard arrived, he gazed at the door and scratched his beard. He performed a magic chant and touched the door to the treasury with his wand, but still the door did not open. "What kind of spell is this that is stronger than your magic, wizard?" asked the king.

The wizard said something that really confused the king: "Only one who is truly innocent can solve this mystery. The solution is carried on the wind, and only one who is pure of heart can listen to it."

The king was distraught, for he did not believe in innocence. He was a wary, skeptical king who had seen much and been disappointed by many. He was convinced that nowhere in his kingdom or in any other kingdom was there someone so pure and capable. If the door could only be opened by an innocent, why then, it could never be opened; the king pronounced it impossible to open. Little did he know that it was he who had endangered his entire kingdom!

Meanwhile bills were piling up with no way to pay them. Guests for the upcoming celebration sent messages of their imminent arrival, but the king knew there would be no food in the pantry to feed them and no exotic gifts to present to them if he did not find a way to open the door to the treasury.

As the king slept that night he had an ominous dream. He dreamed that three men were ravaging his kingdom. The first man was obese and was eating virtually everything in the kingdom that was edible, growing visibly fatter by the minute. The second man was covered with disfiguring open sores that would not heal; wherever he went, everyone fled from him in horror. The third man was a masked bandit who was terrorizing people throughout the land, stealing their money and possessions and leaving them penniless. The king awoke in a sweat in the middle of the night, disturbed by the vision in his dream. He felt it portended some great misfortune but did not know exactly what to make of it. The next morning he called for the royal soothsayer to come to his chamber to interpret the dream.

When the soothsayer arrived, the king recounted his dream in careful detail. "What does this dream mean?" the king asked. "It makes no sense to me, but it leaves me with a feeling of great dread. I'm afraid it may be an omen."

"In truth, your majesty, I believe you will not like what I have to say," said the soothsayer, "but I must tell you that your kingdom will be visited by disaster."

"Just as I feared," said the king. "But what kind of disaster? Can you tell me more?"

"The man who eats too much represents famine and hunger," replied the soothsayer. "Something will threaten the kingdom's food supply, and your people will go hungry if you do not act."

"I see," said the king, looking very puzzled indeed, for as far as he knew, the farms and farmers of his realm were thriving, and he was aware of no immediate threat to the food supply. "And what about the man with the skin malady?" he asked.

"He is sickness and death. Your kingdom will be threatened by a plague," said the soothsayer.

"How can this be?" said the king. "My people are in good health, and we have the finest healers!" The king was becoming very perplexed and began to wonder if he should trust the royal soothsayer. "And what do you make of the masked bandit?" he asked somewhat dubiously.

"Poverty, your majesty." The soothsayer paused, seeming somewhat embarrassed and uncomfortable. He continued hesitantly, "There are problems with money and finances. The people are being deprived of what should be theirs, and they will suffer if this continues."

"Oh, nonsense!" cried the king. "This makes no sense at all!" He dismissed the soothsayer and gave the matter no more thought.

Later that same day, however, the king discovered to his horror that the omens in his dream had come true. Alarming reports came in saying that half the people in his kingdom had suddenly fallen ill with a mysterious disease. Furthermore, locusts had descended on the kingdom's crops and were rapidly decimating them. And as if that weren't enough, the king's creditors were threatening revolt if he did not pay his bills at once.

His mind turned dark, as did his heart. He went once again to the treasury door and tried to open it, but still found it stuck fast. "Life always did deal with me harshly," he thought. "I don't think I can survive this."

When the king awoke the next morning, he felt very ill and worried that the same mysterious illness that was spreading through the kingdom had now afflicted him. He called the royal physician, who predicted the worst. When the king heard this dire prognosis, his condition worsened. He had a raging fever and in his delirium he tossed and turned. The wind heard his moans and knew that he was near death, so it tickled his ear with a name: Florence.

"Florence," the king said weakly, not really understanding why, but feeling suddenly that he needed to see her.

The physician looked at the queen and asked, "Who, pray tell, is Florence?"

Queen Raisa shrugged her shoulders. She knew nobody by that name. The queen and the physician asked the royal census taker if he knew of anyone named Florence.

"No," he said, "I've heard of no woman in this kingdom named Florence."

But the king kept repeating the name, and Queen Raisa thought that perhaps this mysterious woman named Florence held the key to her husband's survival. With his condition worsening rapidly, it became clear that something had to be done, and quickly.

She cast a loving glance at the suffering king and decided to take matters into her own hands. Riding on horseback, she went from village to village to inquire about a woman named Florence. There were many women: Kathryn, Gertrude, Vanessa, Cecilia, and countless others, but no one named Florence.

The queen passed through village after village with no success. After visiting every single village in her husband's kingdom, still there was no woman called Florence to be found. The sun was beginning to set, and soon she would be forced to turn back. She was terribly thirsty and needed a drink before turning around to head back to the castle. As she passed through the very last village, preparing to turn back, she spotted a child smiling at her from the window of a broken-down shack. The child had the most angelic smile the queen had ever seen. The queen was enchanted by the sweet and simple nature of the girl and decided this was as good a place as any to stop for a drink of water. She approached the shack and knocked on the door. The child answered.

"I'm in need of a drink of water, dear child. May I come in?"

The child did not know who she was dealing with, for she had never before seen the queen and did not curtsy, but she gladly offered a cup of water to satisfy her guest's thirst.

The queen asked, "Child, do you know a woman named Florence?"

"No, ma'am, I don't," the girl answered.

This was very discouraging. The queen was losing hope. "What is your name, child?" the queen asked, making a mental note to be sure to remember the name of this friendly girl when she returned to the castle so she could later send a royal thank-you note.

"Florence," she replied.

"But I thought you said you didn't know anyone named Florence!" said the queen.

"You asked me if I knew any *woman* named Florence, Ma'am. I thought you were looking for a grown-up," the girl explained.

"Why, then, I wonder if *you* are who I am looking for?" said the queen, somewhat puzzled. She did not see how a child could possibly be of any use in this situation, yet she was desperate enough to try nearly anything, for there was little to lose at this point. "Florence," she said, "would you ask your mother if you may come with me to the royal castle? The king is very sick, and I believe you can help."

"Of course I will," said Florence. Her mother happily gave her consent for Florence to go, and together the pair rode back to the castle. Florence was brought before the king.

"Florence," he cried out in his fever. "Save me, save us all!"

Florence looked at the queen, who encouraged her with a gentle nudge.

Florence approached the king. "What is it you need me to do, Sir?" she asked.

"Florence, my kingdom is in great danger and nearly at its end," said the king. With great effort, he sat up in bed, feverish and drenched in sweat. "Do you know the answer to what has befallen me and my kingdom? Can you advise me about what to do?" he asked. He really did not expect that she—a mere child, and a girl at that—would be able to solve these perplexing problems, but for the moment he was willing to let her try.

"Sir, all I know is what my mother taught me: that the words we speak become our future when the wind carries them to all the forces of the universe," she told him.

"The wind?" The king asked, unsure of how to interpret the words. Then he remembered what the wizard had told him, that only one who is pure-hearted could listen to the wind. "Can you hear the voice of the wind, Florence? Will it tell you why I've become sick, or why I can't open the door to my treasury?" asked the king.

Florence closed her eyes and listened intently for a long time, not with her ears, but with her heart. She heard the whisper of the wind as it moved through the room, and she heard the faint echoes of the king's own words that had created his affliction.

She opened her eyes and looked at the king. She quietly told him, "You closed the treasury yourself—don't you remember? I heard you say that no one could open the door, and the wind carried your words to the forces of the universe. Then you said you were tired of being the king. The words you spoke became your future. And when you said, 'I don't think I can survive this,' that's when you became sick."

"But what must I do to change all of this?" begged the king.

"Speak words of blessing, your majesty, and your future will change," Florence replied.

King Shevon sat up and pondered this wisdom. Then with all the strength he had in his body, he cried out, "Bless this kingdom and its king!"

Then Queen Raisa, too, took up the cry, "Bless this kingdom and its king!"

Then Florence joined them, saying, "Bless this kingdom and its king!" And the wind carried this chant far and wide across the land, to every valley and hill and every meadow and stream. Almost immediately the king felt some life flowing back into his veins, but still he was not completely well.

"What you have said can't simply be undone with words—it requires *acts* of blessing, too," Florence explained. "You must show kindness and rule with wisdom."

By now the king was sipping some hot chicken soup and was feeling much better. Finishing that, he decided to test his legs to see if he had recovered enough to stand up again. Finding that he could, he called for his cane and asked everyone to follow him to the treasury door.

"Let the door open," he said. He grasped its handle and turned and pulled it, but to his disappointment he found the door still wouldn't budge. "What more must I do to open the treasury?" he asked Florence.

"For this," she told him, "you must perform an act of generosity. Instead of hoarding your riches and possessions, you must give away what you have no need for."

"Hmmm. I have many things that are not being used."
He paused to think on this for a moment. "Captain of the
guards!" he called. "Whatever is not of use to our family, I
wish to dispense to the people of the village." And so it
was done.

Gaining confidence, the king declared, "I take back every
untrue word I have said about life, people, health,
prosperity, and this door! I want those false words to return
to nothing because they arose from the vain imaginings of
my heart. Now and forevermore, I want the wind to spread
my blessings throughout the land."

Florence's heart was filled with love and admiration for
the king. She stood beside him and together they visualized
the door opening. "Bless this door, for it is good," they spoke
to the wind. "Bless this door, for it is a willing servant to
the king. It opens with kindness, it closes with kindness."
Just then, a gentle wind began to blow through the window,
and the door creaked open.

The queen, amazed at what she had seen, asked
Florence, "Child, if you have this great wisdom, why do you
live so humbly?"

"I lived humbly before, but now look!" she said, leading
them outside the castle into view of the nearby village.
The entire village had been transformed. Instead of huts
and shacks, there were beautiful homes. The illness that
had afflicted the people faded, and there were joyful people
making preparations to replant the crops the locusts had
destroyed. Not only that, but a caravan of camels approached, carrying in new supplies to replenish the
decimated food supply. It was truly a paradise!

From that moment on the king, the queen, and everyone in the kingdom were careful to speak only words of truth and blessing. If something went wrong in their lives, they blessed it with their words and deeds and imagined it being set right. If someone wronged them, they blessed the errant one with all the love in their heart and beseeched the forces of the universe to make them as one. And the wind circled the earth with all their blessings!

The Girl
Who Climbed a Ladder
to the Stars

*E*veryone in the village of Tambala knew the prophecy of the ladder to the stars. For as long as anyone could remember, it had been a part of the village lore. As the legend went, the sky and the earth had once been the same, but one day they fought and split into two: the sky above and the earth below. As the legend said, they would only be reunited when someone climbed a ladder to the stars, which would bring peace and prosperity to everyone. For centuries the story had been told, but no one had any idea of how they might build such a ladder.

Nevertheless, the people of Tambala built ladders as tall and far-reaching as they could make them. They were awkward, wavering structures that men climbed, trying to figure out how to get the ladders ever-higher. Ladders became a precious thing to the people of the village, and even a tiny three-rung ladder was almost a sacred object.

One thing was clear, though: women were not allowed to climb the ladders. Mother Earth was a woman, they said, and so it made sense for a woman's place to be firmly on the ground. Not only were men the only ones who could reach for the stars, they did whatever work required a ladder, for they believed women were not capable of such things. The women did the cooking, sewing, cleaning, and tending to the babies and children, for it made no sense to expose those who bore the children to the risks of ladder climbing.

However, there was a young girl named Maya in the village who was different from the other girls her age. From her earliest years she had shown evidences of an unnatural, perverse, and worrisome interest in climbing. Somehow at two years of age Maya had managed to climb into a tree and could not get down. Her parents had certainly frowned upon this, and she received a scolding. Her parents understood from this that they would have to be extra vigilant in training and protecting their daughter from her own dangerous tendencies. Though she learned by trial and error which behaviors and interests were acceptable and which were not, as she grew older the desire to climb and to see things from a different vantage point intensified within her. She developed a fascination with ladders.

At age twelve Maya had learned never to let it be known that she was interested in climbing, but her fascination with ladders was growing. She had been watching the men and the boys of the village building a hut for a newly married couple. The basic structure was up, and the walls had been completed. On this particular day, as soon as they finished their noon meal, the men of Tambala were going to thatch the roof and finish the hut. This, of course, would involve working on ladders. The men would be climbing up high and doing dangerous but necessary work. Maya was avidly waiting to watch this exciting activity.

Maya was ladling out soup to the men, listening to their conversation about the work that lay ahead. When she filled the last bowl of soup, she stepped aside to wait as the men ate. No one was watching her. Had they been paying attention, they would have seen her looking longingly at the ladder. She couldn't keep her eyes off of it, for it was like a magnet to her, drawing her nearer, pulling her toward it.

She cautiously moved closer to the object of her fascination. When she was right next to the ladder, she carefully put her foot on the first rung, for she thought no one was looking. She began to imagine what it might be like to climb its rungs and stand at the top and behold the scene from there. Even though it was only a few feet high, she delighted at the thought of the different perspective it would give her on things in the village. What would the world look like from there? She imagined herself atop the ladder and let her mind wander to the tallest ladder in Tambala. What would it be like to be higher than anything else in the village, she wondered.

She was musing on this tantalizing thought when a boy named Phoenix spotted her and yelled out, "Look at the girl who would climb the ladder! Get away from there!"

All eyes turned to look at her in shock.

Maya felt deeply ashamed and ran. She ran to her favorite hiding place in the forest outside the village and wept under her favorite tree.

Why do I have to be so different? she thought as she cried. Why can't I be a normal girl who wants to do normal things? What's wrong with me? Oh, who wants to climb a ladder anyway? It's dangerous and foolish, and no one will ever want anything to do with me if I break the rules. As she sat and sobbed, a voice spoke to her that seemed to be coming from the very ground she sat on.

"Are you brave enough to climb a ladder?" it asked.

"Who is that?" Maya asked, startled.

"I'm Mother Earth," said the voice.

Maya knew it must be true because the voice sounded like the echoes of chirping birds and the wind through the trees. Mother Earth told her, "I believe the time has come to rejoin what was split, and for that to happen, I need you to climb a ladder. Are you brave enough?"

"Girls don't climb ladders," Maya said defiantly. But Mother Earth had watched the girl grow up and knew of her fascination with the ladders, forbidden or not.

"What if you had a chance to climb a ladder to the stars?" Mother Earth asked.

"A ladder to the stars? That's ridiculous!" said Maya. "Even if it were possible, why would I want to do it?"

Mother Earth answered, "So you can see what the stars see and fulfill your destiny!"

"But what good will that do me?" Maya asked. "The people of Tambala will have nothing to do with me if I do it. I would be shunned! I don't want to see what the stars see if I have to spend the rest of my life alone. I just want to be normal! Why can't I be like other girls? What's wrong with me?"

"You must follow your heart, Maya. Only a girl who is brave and courageous and strong will climb the ladder and see what the stars see," said Mother Earth. "It is your destiny."

Maya contemplated this for a moment. The thought of seeing what the stars see was alluring, but how could it be possible? Even if it could be done, she feared what would happen if anyone were to find out, and she was very worried about safety.

"Who would hold the ladder for me?" she asked. "Everyone knows that girls don't have the strength to climb ladders. It takes extraordinary skill and balance. No woman has ever done it before, and if I fall it will be the end of me!"

"I will hold the ladder for you," said Mother Earth.

"But there aren't any ladders tall enough to reach the stars," she said.

"You would have to trust me," said Mother Earth. "A bird must build his nest in faith. A farmer must plant his field in faith, and a hunter must shoot his arrow in faith."

"What does that have to do with this?" said Maya, starting to move away. But when she tried to take her first step, she found she was unable to move her feet. She looked down and saw that Mother Earth had instantly woven an intricate pair of sandals out of the tall grasses around her feet. Her feet were firmly rooted to the ground! "How did you do that?" she said in astonishment.

"I told you I would hold the ladder! I am Mother Earth! Wood and grass and stone are all a part of me."

And because Maya couldn't move her feet, she came to see that many things she had thought impossible might indeed be possible. If Mother Earth could stop her in her tracks like that, then maybe climbing a ladder to the stars wasn't impossible. She would trust Mother Nature and give it a try.

Maya remained in the forest and waited until darkness fell. Then she quietly returned to the village, headed for the one place where she knew she was likely to find a ladder: the newlyweds' hut. Just as she had thought, the ladder was still there. The men of the village had left it leaning against the newly constructed hut at the end of the work day.

She knew she shouldn't, for she was only a girl. She knew she couldn't, for it was against the rules of the village. But if not now, when?

She took a deep breath and quickly moved to the ladder. Stepping onto the first rung, her heart pounding, she quickly climbed to the second and third rungs. She paused there, for she heard a noise behind her.

It was the boy named Phoenix, who had spotted her earlier that day with her foot on the first rung. He was coming out of his hut. He saw her on the ladder and yelled, "Stop the girl! She's climbing the ladder! She's going to get hurt!" He leaped out of his hut, running as fast as he could. But as soon as his feet touched the ground, Mother Earth laced them firmly to the ground with the tall grasses. He fell face-first, with his hands just inches from the ladder, and Mother Earth quickly wrapped his wrists and hands against the earth.

"Help me, help me!" he yelled, "Maya is climbing the ladder! Somebody do something!"

Maya was terrified and froze for a moment in place, her foot poised midway between the third and fourth rung.

One by one the men and women of Tambala came out of their huts to see what was the matter. As soon as they attempted to move toward Maya to stop her, Mother Earth tied their feet to the ground.

The men of the village began to berate the young girl: "Who do you think you are? Get down from that ladder before you hurt yourself! You know the rules of the village. Get down from there right now!"

Then the women started shouting at her: "Get down from there, you stupid creature! You are bringing great shame upon our village! Women cannot climb ladders. That's men's work! Stop trying to change everything! Don't you know your place? You'll hurt yourself! Get down from there immediately before we beat you!"

The girl began to shake in fear on the ladder, and she stopped believing in herself. "Oh, Mother Earth, what should I do? Maybe this is all wrong!"

Mother Earth said, "Can you feel the rungs beneath your feet? Can you feel them in your hands?"

"Yes, I can," said Maya.

"Can you picture yourself climbing the rungs in your mind?"

"Yes, I can!" said Maya.

"Then don't listen to them! Just go!"

And up she went. Maya climbed to the fourth rung, and the fifth rung, and the sixth, and when she got her hands on the seventh and eighth rungs she thought, "I hope there's more after this one!" And when she reached for another, there it was—strong, fresh green wood with bright green leaves and vines climbing straight up to the sky.

The girl climbed as high as the trees, and when she looked down, she saw the whole village looking up at her. They were glaring at her in anger, concern, and bewilderment. They could not believe what they were seeing.

Maya looked down, filled with excitement. She was disappointed that everyone was so angry at her, but now that she was on the ladder she could see that there was no harm in it. She wished they could all see what she saw, for she knew that they would change their minds if they had the chance. She said, "This is my family, and I love them and bless them even though they tried to stop me."

She climbed as high as the clouds, and when she looked as far as she could see to the east, she saw Asian fishermen on the horizon out for the day's catch of fish. She saw that they had a great concern for their children and that they worked just as hard as the men and women of her village. They were people of great skill and ingenuity, and she felt overwhelming love for them. "This, too, is my family. I never knew they were there before, but I see them now, and I feel very close to them," she thought as she climbed higher.

Meanwhile, Mother Earth had plans for Phoenix, who was flat on the ground. The grass that bound his limbs released him, and he quickly jumped to a crouching position and sprang to the ladder, climbing to the top of the roofs. He smiled down at the people of his village, for this was his home and these were his people. Then he scrambled up the ladder after the girl to stop her and to save her from herself! He had powerful legs and arms and was moving very fast.

Maya was already as high as the highest mountains and paused to look to the south. She saw dark-skinned peoples who had great dignity and intelligence. They were struggling to care for their families just like the people of her village. A wave of tenderness washed over her heart. "Oh, I want these people to be part of my family, too!" she exclaimed as she climbed higher.

Meanwhile the young man had climbed to the clouds, and he was gazing on the beauty of the Asian peoples. He had never known that there were other people beyond the boundaries of his land and his imagination. As he looked at them, he had strange feelings that conflicted with his training as a warrior, particularly when he saw the children. He must stop these feelings, but first he must stop Maya!

She had climbed to the zenith of the sky and was looking to the north. There she saw a hard-working group of pale-skinned people living in a very cold climate, toiling vigorously to provide for their families under difficult conditions. She wept for the nobility that she could see was in their hearts and minds. "My family is growing greater and greater. I love these people, too. I want them to be part of my family as well," she said as she climbed higher.

Now Phoenix was speeding upwards rapidly and turned to look toward the south. He, too, saw the dark-skinned peoples and their children. He saw their dignity and strength, and he began to wonder what all of this meant. Could it be that they, too, were like the people of his village? But he knew he mustn't let these thoughts sway him from his task. "I must stop Maya," he said, breathing heavily from the exertion of climbing as he reached for the next rungs of the ladder.

Climbing higher, he looked to the north and saw the pale-skinned people and could not help feeling the same urge to weep as Maya had felt when he watched them toiling to feed and care for their families. He knew not what was overcoming him, but it was making him see and feel things he had never felt before. Shaking himself and coming to his senses again, he remembered he must go on to stop Maya, and he continued his climb in great haste, determined to catch her.

Maya arrived at the stars with Phoenix at her heels, and she looked to the west. There she saw a group of bronze-skinned people who lived in harmony with the earth and appeared to have great knowledge of all creation. Maya was deeply touched by their way of life and marveled at their beauty.

Maya and Phoenix now realized that the wondrous, brilliant, sparkling stars were shining in the firmament all around them. Maya looked down from her place on the ladder and said, "Mother Earth is just one great village of the great family of man!" The boy nodded in agreement, surveying the four directions and admiring his great family all around him.

"What will happen now?" he asked. "Will the sky and the earth become joined again?"

"Can't you see?" Maya said, pointing to the globe floating amidst the darkness. "They're together and they always have been. Just like all the people of all the villages. We thought that they were separate, but they're only one village. And even as the women weren't allowed to climb the ladder, yet here I am—the men and the women of Tambala are just different parts of the same family, too."

They heard Mother Earth's voice speak to them. "Now you understand," she said. "The ladder has allowed you both to see the truth, and now that message will allow the people in all the villages reach their true purpose."

The two consulted about what to do next. How could they return to the village and resume their lives as before? It was unthinkable, out of the question. They would never be the same. But still they wanted to tell the story of what they'd seen.

Maya had an idea. "We could climb back down the ladder and go from village to village and tell the story of the different-colored children of the world. Or we could leap from this ladder and stay for eternity to dance among the stars, and shine the truth from the night sky."

They decided to stay and dance among the stars. They let go of the ladder, taking one more look at Mother Earth shimmering in blue and green. They felt such a love and longing in their hearts for Mother Earth that they dove toward her with their arms outstretched. And as they dove through the sky, they turned into two shooting stars. Mother Earth saw their shimmering trails of starlight tracing across the sky and knew they would blaze for eternity.

So when you go out at night and see the dark starry sky, look for those two shooting stars and gather up the stardust in their trails. Then sprinkle it on the hearts of all humankind so that hearts everywhere may see the true unity and equality of Maya and Phoenix!

6

The Wall of Sorrows

*T*he men of the village of Sorrono were known throughout their lands as the strongest and most cunning warriors. With each battle they waged on the surrounding villages and towns, they collected the spoils of victory. Gold was piled up in the treasuries and given to the people of the village. Though the constant fighting cost the lives of many young men of the village, it was important for them to be the richest and most powerful village in the land.

But as the men plundered successive villages, they were forced to venture farther and farther away to find more treasures. Eventually the men were gone so long that the women of the village began to wonder if they would ever return.

When they did return, slowly filtering back into the village, there were many dead and wounded. Some had been buried at the site of battle, some had been buried during the long journey home. The walking wounded limped along with the assistance of others while those who were unable to walk were carried on litters. All were suffering. Yet at the front of the procession were those who carried the spoils of war, the treasures that were to keep the village rich and prosperous.

The women rushed up to meet the men as they approached the village. They each looked for their loved ones. The children ran ahead of the women, looking for their fathers, brothers, and uncles. Those who were fortunate soon clasped each other tightly, tears of gratitude running down their faces. Many were not as fortunate. They looked, but their loved ones were lost to them forever. In all, half of the men were gone—half of the brothers, half of the fathers, half of the uncles.

All of the women had lost some family member, and all of them wept bitterly. When they realized how great the losses were, the grief-stricken women ran, blinded by tears, to the centuries-old Wall of Sorrows that stood at the edge of the village. The Wall of Sorrows was a hallowed place, an ancient gray stone wall, tall and curved like a horseshoe, where the women unburdened themselves from the losses brought on by the constant warring. The women wailed at the wall and beat their chests. They screamed out their woes, and the Wall of Sorrows comforted them. It took in the sounds of their sorrow and gently echoed the sorrow back to them in wave after wave of lamenting that was like a balm to their hearts. Century after century the women gathered in front of the great Wall of Sorrows, and they knew they would continue to do so century upon century into the future.

But the number of women crowding into the shadow of the wall was greater this time than ever before. The women's cries were so loud, and the echoes so numerous, that each woman could barely hear her own voice. Instead, it was a cacophonous wash of tearful voices. The echoes were less comforting this time. A dark mist rose around the women as their sorrows hung in the air around them, too dense to dissipate, steadily building with each woman's pain.

The children of the village hid behind trees and bushes and rocks and watched the women wail. They too were sad and wanted to help their mothers, and sisters, and aunts, and grandmothers, but the aura of pain surrounding the women and the wall intimidated them. So they watched and listened, whispering amongst themselves. They wondered: Why do our fathers, and brothers, and uncles, and grandfathers go to war? Why don't they stop seeking treasure from other villages? No treasure is worth losing our fathers, or brothers, or uncles, or grandfathers.

The men also watched the women at the Wall of Sorrows from a distance. They waited for a month, as was the custom, before they brought the treasures gained in the war and placed them in front of the women, who still shivered beneath the Wall of Sorrows and the fog that had arisen. As they approached, though, there was none of the calm that they expected. Instead, the women looked even more harried and distraught than before they had come to the wall. The women's voices were hoarse from crying out their sorrows at such length, yet they remained at the wall, searching for the comfort they had come to expect, not knowing where else to turn.

The chief of the village signaled to the other men to stay back. He reached into one of the baskets full of treasure and took out a beautiful golden bracelet that he raised into the air. His thought was that the sight of the treasures would revive the women's spirits and alleviate their sorrows.

He came closer and offered the bracelet to his wife, Noelani, who wearily took it. Attending to custom, she looked into another basket and pulled out a treasure for her sister. Her sister took it. Then the sister took a treasure out of the basket and handed it to her aunt. And so the spoils of war were dispersed amongst the women of the village.

Everyone grew silent before the Wall of Sorrows as they examined their individual treasures. The children spied from behind their hiding places. They didn't understand the reasons for war, but knew that the treasures were important. A twelve-year-old girl, Nova, whose mother stood among the grieving women, asked, "Is that why there is war? So we can have treasures and have a wealthy tribe?"

She followed the men as they returned to the village. They gathered far from the Wall of Sorrows to talk about the war they had fought: "They were different than we are." "They believed differently than we do—they worshiped a different God." "They thought they were superior to us, but we showed them." "They wanted to take part of our land." "Did you see how different their eyes were? Did you see the cast of their skin?" "We must remain the strongest and wealthiest village, or we too will fall. Now that we've lost so many men of the village, we must seek others who look like us and think like us to join with us so we can grow stronger and stronger." They talked like this for hours. There were so many different reasons for fighting that Nova wondered whether the men really did know why they went to war.

Back at the Wall of Sorrows, the women began to compare their treasures one with another. Some women had greater treasures and others had lesser treasures. Envy began to creep into one woman's heart. One woman eyed a necklace that another woman had received. She waited until the woman turned around so that she could take it away from her. She quickly stepped into the shadows of a tree near where the children were watching and hid herself.

Another woman began to be jealous of the other women who still had husbands. Who was going to take care of her? Who was going to bring her treasures from the next war? She began to question the leadership of the village. The only one among the villagers who really prospered was Noelani, the chief's wife. She always got the best treasures, and she didn't have to share with the others. And furthermore, her husband, the chief, was never on the front line of the battles, so he always returned from war safely. It was the chief's wife who wanted the men to go to war. So it was the chief's wife who was responsible for this woman's loss.

"It's your husband's fault that my husband is dead," she yelled out.

"You can't talk about my husband that way!" insisted Noelani.

"You think you're superior because you're the wife of the chief, but you're not!"

Noelani's sister stood up to defend her. "You can't talk to my sister that way!" she yelled, and slapped the other woman and called her an ugly name. The name echoed off the Wall of Sorrows. So did the sound of the woman's hand slapping across the face of the woman filled with jealousy and bitterness.

Two other women began to talk to each other, "What do you think about what she said about the chief's wife?" Such a chatter they began! Then they all began to talk about the jealous woman in front of her.

Another woman yelled out, "You stupid woman, you have no right to slap her!" The words echoed off the Wall of Sorrows.

Then there was another outburst between three other women. More hurtful names were shouted, and the Wall of Sorrows echoed each of them. Gossip began to spring up amongst the many women who were questioning the character of others.

Nova returned to her hiding place among the other children, who were now shivering and crying as they watched their mothers and sisters viciously attack each other. The sadness from the Wall of Sorrows had hurt them, but now they were terrified.

The women's struggle became a violent war fought with words. They tried to bite each other with words. Others attempted to slap their former friends with ugly names. The women began to separate into groups, aligning against each other. They bristled at women whom they now considered enemies, demeaning them as they began to bring up things from the past, reopening wounds that had never healed and raging about mistakes and flaws that had never been forgiven.

Their collective rage began to grow, and the cloud that had seemed to descend around the women began to turn into a hot, foul wind. At that moment, half of the women became silent. Those who were silent wondered why the raging was so deafeningly loud. The raging women saw fear on the faces of the silent women and they became silent. Still the sound of rage continued. They looked at the wall. It was roaring! The Wall of Sorrows had now become the Wall of Rage.

The echoes would not stop reverberating. Wave after wave of rage poured forth, viciously pummeling the frightened women standing in front of it. The hearts of some of the women were turning to stone, and their faces were beginning to twist into grotesque masks that were as ugly and violent as the curses they hurled at each other. One of the women picked up a spear, and with a violent thrust began to threaten another woman.

The children were extremely fearful now. They looked at each other in terror, fearing for the safety of their mothers and aunts and grandmothers.

Nova rushed into the village to summon the men, who were still discussing their latest victory. "You must come quickly," she told them. "Something has happened at the Wall of Sorrows, and all the women are being attacked."

The men gathered their swords and bows and spears and rushed to the wall. But when they arrived they were perplexed by the scene. They didn't know what to do—they couldn't raise their swords against their own wives, sisters, and mothers. Yet as they approached the wall, echoes of rage began to reach into their hearts as well. Their eyes flashed with anger and violence, and they readied their weapons.

Nova knew that she had to do something. She waded into the midst of the women, ignoring the echoes and the hot wind that bit at her skin and whipped her hair. She was brave, and her love for the people of the village overcame her fear. She knew that love was the only thing that could dispel the violence. She ran into the fray and began to shout at the wall but found that her voice was lost amidst the awful clamor that the rage had created.

Quickly, she ran back to the children and gathered them around her, telling them that they must join her. "I know you're afraid," she said, "but we have to do something to save our village." Inspired by her courage, the other children followed her, emerging from behind trees and bushes and rocks. They approached the women and placed themselves between the women and the Wall of Rage.

Then, following Nova's direction, the children faced the wall and began to say kind things about all the people of the village, offering blessings and gratitude to their mothers, sisters, and aunts: "You've always been such a wonderful cook." "You're so kind and gentle." "Your wonderful stories have always made me happy." "I always feel safe when I am with you." "Thank you for taking care of me when I was sick." "Thank you for teaching me how to fish." Most importantly, they kept repeating the message: "I love you."

The Wall of Rage continued to rage, and tears streamed from the children's faces, but Nova urged them to continue. So they kept saying kind things and offering prayers of thanks and praise. Slowly but surely, the Wall of Rage began to quiet its rumbling and roaring, and the wind began to falter, as every so often a word of kindness would echo from the Wall of Rage. The longer the children continued saying kind things, the quieter the wall became.

Soon echoes of kindness began to penetrate the hearts of the women, and they began to remember the kindnesses they had shown one another in the past. Then they began to remember that they loved all the other women of the village, and they realized once again that they believed in the goodness of each other. One by one, the women turned to the wall and began to say kind things, until the wind of rage was gone and the fog of sadness was gone, and what remained was a warm light that radiated from the echoes of kindness.

That light and those echoes floated over the men, and their thoughts of war became confused by the influence of the wall and the sounds of kindness that surrounded them. First one man, then another, began to say kind things. Words of kindness became mixed with words of war. The men looked strangely at one another because the words of war didn't match the feelings of kindness.

All were surrounded by kind hearts and kind thoughts and kind words and kind echoes. The men's weapons clattered to the ground, and the people of the village embraced each other. There were treasures—the spoils of their wars, littering the ground, but all of them seemed dull and dusty compared to the warmth they felt reflecting back at them from the wall. What use were these treasures when they could all find something so wonderful without the need for violence, sadness, and loss?

The Wall of Rage became known as the Wall of Kindness. As the years went on, the people of the village continued to speak kind words to the wall as well as to each other. The village became famous throughout the land not for its fierce warriors but for its great generosity and warmth.

Whenever someone among them was burdened with sadness, the other villagers would aid that person with kind and sweet words that would echo from the Wall of Kindness and become a blessing to all.

7

The Quest
on the
Holy Mountain

*T*he king frowned and held his head as he sat on his throne. Though his was only one kingdom among many, the whole world seemed to be facing disaster: Famine was widespread, money was devalued, governments succumbed to anarchy, centuries-old temples were falling apart and the faithful wandered disillusioned and estranged, and armies were powerless to right the many wrongs that were being committed.

King Sadiki was a just and wise king, and seeing his kingdom in such travail was a burden on his heart. But none of the counselors and sages he consulted gave him the answers he sought. They, too, seemed lost in the mire that was engulfing the world.

Yet he knew that there was at least one person in his kingdom who still had hope: his daughter, Janeal. King Sadiki did not know where her inspiration came from, but if she had some clue as to how to solve the problems of the kingdom, he would listen.

"Father, I have an idea," she told him. "Let us go to the Holy Mountain. According to legend, whoever climbs it with a pure heart will be rewarded with his heart's desire."

"But, my dear, no one has been able to approach that peak, not for generations. Everyone who has tried has failed and turned back," the king reminded his daughter.

"But that's no reason not to try," she responded. "You've tried everything else, and all of the wisest people in the kingdom can find no better solution. What have we got to lose?"

"So be it. There will be a quest for the Holy Mountain and whatever knowledge is contained there. But who should I send?"

"Father, you must send the wisest of the wise—those who have the knowledge of all the kingdom. Send the Sage and the Doctor," she said.

"Of course," said the king, "but we must also have those who are the bravest of the brave."

"Certainly the Knight and the Woodsman would be brave and strong—able to confront any physical obstacle," she added. "And you will need those with great vision as well."

"For that I shall send the Poet, and the Teacher," said the king, warming to the idea of the quest and slowly allowing himself to grow hopeful. "There is one other requirement, though—they need a leader who is pure in heart."

"And who should that be?" asked his daughter.

"The one person who has hope when all others have lost it," he replied and smiled proudly at her.

"Me?" she asked. "But Father, I'm not wise or strong, and I don't have great vision."

"I believe that you must go," he said emphatically. "This plan is your doing, and I believe you have a special role to play in it. The quest must begin as soon as possible. It shall begin tomorrow."

She agreed to her father's wishes, and as he set about assembling the party to make the quest, she went to her room to prepare in her own way. That night Janeal said a prayer that the wind carried to the Holy Mountain. She closed her eyes and uttered a powerful affirmation: "I vow to God and to myself that no matter what happens on this quest I will climb the Holy Mountain with a pure and radiant heart!"

The next morning the group assembled and began the trek to the foot of the Holy Mountain. It was a difficult trip, not only because of the distance they had to travel but also because as they journeyed, they witnessed the suffering that had overtaken the lands. They could hear the despairing cries of the people of the kingdom and saw the hopelessness in their eyes. Some of them were homeless; some of them were sick and in great pain. "Please help us," they cried.

Sadness filled the young girl's heart. She reached out and touched the hand of a frightened, weeping child who had been orphaned. "Please don't be frightened," she said. "We are on a quest to seek the answers to the world's problems. And when we find them, we will return and put right everything in the kingdom."

When they set down camp on the first night, they had made it halfway to the foot of the mountain. It soon became clear that the king's champions did not get along. Each man had been chosen for his particular skill, but each wanted to establish his superiority instead of working as a member of the group. Each one secretly thought himself and his methods better than the others and made it plain that he would not be influenced by an inferior.

They all implored different spirits and offered various prayers that the others thought strange and superstitious. When the Woodsman implored the trees to guide them, the Knight silently scoffed. And when the Poet called on his muses for assistance, the Sage thought perhaps he was a madman.

The next morning they argued, and the conflict continued until they reached the base of the mountain. They could not agree on how to begin the climb. The Woodsman thought they should proceed through the forest, since many had tried to ascend the trail before and had been forced to turn back. The Poet thought they should wait until inspiration struck them. The Sage brought out arcane maps that he said showed a secret way that no one had ever tried before.

But the king's daughter summoned them all together. She had been appointed as their leader and so she was the one to make the final choice.

"We shall take the trail," she said. "Sometimes the way that's marked is the best."

So they set off together on the trail, but the Woodsman grumbled inwardly. What use was he if they were on the trail, he thought. His talents were needed in the thicket and through the forests. His skills were being wasted on the trail, and in all likelihood, they would have to turn back and go through the forest anyway.

The climb grew more difficult as they made progress. The incline of the mountain became steeper and the path rockier and more uneven. Sweat dampened their brows and poured down their backs as they struggled in the afternoon sun. They were nearly a quarter of the way up the mountain when the Sage balked on the trail and insisted it was time to turn back.

"What's the matter?" asked Janeal. "The pathway is clear."

"That's an insurmountable barrier," he replied, pointing to a small wooden structure that looked like some sort of shrine. It was decorated with various runes, and scrolls and books were stuffed in its alcoves. "It's a shrine to the knowledge of the ancients, and it means that all of the knowledge of the ancients has been revealed, for there is nothing that we need to know beyond this marker. Anything more will only lead to confusion."

"Surely this can't be the end," she protested, "for there must be a way to gain new knowledge."

The Sage would not listen. "We must not pass beyond this point," he insisted as he retreated down the mountain.

But the others remained steadfast on the path and even felt themselves swell with pride. The Sage was now gone, but the remaining heroes counted themselves as all the more brave and wise. They climbed in silence for another two hours when suddenly the Teacher stopped.

"Thus far and no farther," said he, pointing to a crystalline structure built by the side of the path.

"What is it?" cried Janeal.

"This is the temple of the Father," stated the Teacher, "and these symbols indicate that the Father's teaching is complete. There is nothing more for us to learn here—we should turn back. There can be nothing more on this mountain."

"But we need you," she wept, and he began to descend the mountain. Her group of six champions was now four, but she was determined to lead them the rest of the way. She wiped away her tears and urged the group on.

They soldiered on until they saw a metal structure adorned with swords. It was the temple of war, and the Knight stopped in his tracks, preparing to abandon his fellow travelers.

"This is the temple of strength," he said. "Its presence on the Holy Mountain means that we can only succeed through our physical prowess. This is the message of the mountain—this is what we must tell the king when we return."

"But there's so much farther to go until we reach the summit," said Janeal. "This can't be the end, can it?"

But the Knight would not hear it, and he set off on his way down the mountain.

The group continued on the path as the sunlight began to dwindle. Though they had covered a great deal of ground, Janeal wondered if they were really any closer to the goal. Only three of her champions were left now—the Doctor, the Woodsman, and the Poet. She looked at them, hoping they would remain and wondering what she might do if they did not.

The next barrier they encountered was a set of pillars made of bone. This time it was the Doctor who said, "I cannot tolerate this expedition. I must turn back. This is too great a barrier."

"But it's only bones!" said Janeal. "What are you afraid of?"

"Don't you see?" he said. "These bones mean that there is nothing more to us than our bodies. There is no wisdom on this mountain except that we are mere mortals. This is all there is. This is the message of the Holy Mountain." He turned his back on her tearful face and disappeared down the path behind them as the party was cut yet again, leaving only Janeal, the Woodsman, and the Poet.

Darkness fell, and with only the moonlight to illuminate the path, their movement was very slow. It was slower still because the path grew steeper and more treacherous. Then, obscuring their only light, clouds began to form in the sky, and soon it began to rain, making the already dark and dangerous path slippery.

There was a brilliant flash of lightning and a groan from the Woodsman. "Here it is," he cried. Before them was a copse of trees whose branches were intertwined. "It is a symbol of my worship," he explained. "This is what we're meant to see on the Holy Mountain. I should have known all along that my own path was the right one. This is where our paths must part."

Janeal protested, but her cries were lost amidst the rain and the thunder as she watched the Woodsman depart alone into the trees.

She was terribly weary from the journey, but somehow she kept moving, putting one foot in front of the other. She could not bear to disappoint her father, the king, nor could she fail the suffering people she had met along the way, for she had promised to put things right. Now she and the Poet were left to complete the task and reach the goal. She looked at him with hope in her heart as they struggled up the arduous path. She could see now that the summit was close enough to be in view, and she was glad at least that she still had one companion.

They had been climbing all through the night, and as dawn broke, they saw another obstacle on the path. It was an archway made of mirrors.

"Aha!" the Poet called out. "This symbol is what we are looking for. This is a sign from the spirits telling us that we already have the knowledge within us. We need only gaze into our own hearts, and we'll find what we seek." He smiled at his insight and turned to go.

"But we're so close to the summit," she said. "We've got to keep going. We can't stop now! Think of the people—who will save the people?"

Physically drained by the long journey up the mountain and exhausted by the sadness in her heart, Janeal sank to her knees.

"Oh, Father, I have failed you," she cried out. Yet as the words left her lips, she saw a flash of light on the mountaintop that obscured even the dawning sunlight. It burst forth in a brilliant dancing pattern that cast an array of colors upon the clouds above her. She could see the summit and knew now that she could reach it, but without her companions, would she know what to do once she was there?

She took one last look back down the mountain, to the world below that was ruined and destitute, then she climbed the last few rocks to the top of the mountain with an urgency she had never felt before.

She finished her climb and knelt humbly upon the Holy Mountain. Soon images of the different forces operating in the world surrounded her. She saw that the barriers that her companions had not been able to overcome were all interconnected, but each could only perceive his part and was blinded to the whole.

Before her bloomed a vision of peace in the world that came from equality and respect, from morality restored and poverty and ignorance banished. She saw the healing of humankind, and her heart was full. Then she raised her arms to the heavens and cried out, "Oh, please, let it be. Let it be!" Then a voice exclaimed, "Blessed be the child who comes to the Holy Mountain with a pure and radiant heart."

She felt her heart would burst, and she knew she had finally found the end to her quest. She turned back down the path, eager to share what she had learned with her father and with the rest of the kingdom. As she ventured forth, she found her comrade the Poet still lingering on the path, somewhat lost. She told him what she had seen and felt at the top of the Holy Mountain, and her fervor was so apparent that he knew she had found something wonderful. As the two walked, they found others—the Doctor, the Knight, the Woodsman, and the Teacher, all still wandering on the path.

To each of them she described the vision of her heart, and upon hearing of it and seeing her newfound radiance, each realized that what he had seen before was simply a barrier—the totems on the path were merely obstacles that had kept them from seeing the oneness that bound them all together. Each man, instead of being fixated on his own path, now saw that all paths lead to this same, single source. This, they came to realize, was the message of the

Holy Mountain. This was the message that would put things right. But it had taken the pure heart of Janeal to enable them to achieve their task and realize this truth.

When they finally reached the foot of the mountain, they found the Sage, sitting under a tree and reading from his many scrolls. He was delighted to see the others, and when they all told him of what had been atop the Holy Mountain, the party was whole once again. Now every corner, every tree, every rock of the Holy Mountain was illumined.

The group passed among the people at the foot of the mountain, and told others of the Mountain's message of unity. Oneness began to spread across the land and then spread to other lands and peoples. As the message spread, amazing changes began to take place. The rich began to share their wealth with the poor, and people whose hearts were filled with hatred turned to love. King Sadiki had been wise to listen to his daughter. His kingdom prospered. And the vision of peace that had been found on the mountaintop blossomed into a reality in the valleys below.

8

The Princess and the Troublesome Dragon

*T*here once was a young princess named Clarice, who lived in a castle with her mother, the queen. The queen was known throughout the land for her kindness and wisdom, and she was careful to raise her daughter to someday serve as a fitting heir to the throne.

The princess wanted to prove to her mother that she was wise and kind enough to rule someday, and she knew that the best way to do it was to prove that she could control a dragon. Dragons were mischievous creatures with terrible tempers and could be quite dangerous, but Clarice was determined to have one for a pet and prove herself to her mother.

"Dragons can be very naughty and troublesome," the queen warned. "They get into everything."

"Oh, they're not so naughty," said the princess. "I will take care of it and make it behave."

There were some mighty warriors who kept dragons as pets, but they were only able to do so because they cut off the dragons' tails and wings. Even then, the dragons would not behave. But the queen did not believe in such violence and did not want her daughter to be cruel to the dragon. Despite their mischief, dragons were still noble, as were all living creatures.

"How will you control it?" the queen asked.

Her daughter replied, "I won't have to use a sword or a lance, Mother. I can be kind to the dragon and make him be good instead of mischievous. All I have to do is make him promise. So please, please, please can I have a dragon for a pet?"

The queen was concerned, but she decided to trust her daughter. "I will allow it, but you must control the dragon. If it ever becomes unruly, then I will give you to the count of three to make your dragon behave," the queen explained.

The princess thanked her mother and set out from the castle the next day to find a dragon. She set out to the west and climbed to the top of the highest hill and yelled, "Dragon, dragon, beast of bone, come and live with me at home!"

She looked to the east but saw no dragons approach. She repeated, "Dragon, dragon, beast of bone, come and live with me at home!" She looked to the west, but still she saw nothing. Again she yelled, "Dragon, dragon, beast of bone, come and live with me at home!" Finally she heard the beat of dragon wings in the distance and saw a dragon appear in the sky, summoned by her words. He was slightly larger than a human and covered in blue scales.

The beast descended upon the young princess. He examined her, and, thinking that she looked kind, decided to listen to what she had to say.

"You want me to come and live with you?" asked the dragon. He was wary. He knew other dragons had been captured by knights who treated them cruelly and knew that he needed to secure her promise to keep his safety.

"Yes, I do. If you come and live with me in the royal castle as my pet, I will care for you," said Clarice.

"Do you promise to feed me all that I can eat?" asked the dragon.

"I promise," answered the young princess.

"And do you promise that you will give me a comfortable bed to sleep in?" he asked.

"I promise," she said.

"And will you promise not to harm me?" asked the dragon.

"I promise—my mother taught me never to hit a living creature, not man or animal!" said the princess.

"Then I will consent to live with you," said the dragon. He consented because he knew a promise from a princess was a very sacred thing.

"Great," said Clarice, "but I need a promise from you, too. You must promise to behave."

"I promise," the dragon said, and opened his mouth into a toothy grin. He knew that living with the princess would be a more comfortable life than he was used to, but he had no intention of keeping his promise. He knew that because he didn't need to fear mistreatment, he could behave however he liked, so he landed in the mud next to the princess, splashing her. She thought perhaps that was only an accident, so she let it go.

The pair returned to the castle and as soon as they were within the gates, the dragon lifted himself up and flew towards the courtyard, landing on a clothesline where clothes were hanging out to dry. Great globs of mud dripped from his claws all over the clean clothes.

The queen saw the muddy dragon from a window and yelled, "One!" Clarice and the dragon looked up at the tower window.

"Oh, naughty dragon!" cried the princess. "Won't you please be nice?"

"You gave your word that you wouldn't hurt me," said the dragon. "So there's nothing you can do to stop me." He laughed. The princess scowled. She had been betrayed, but she still knew a secret that would help her if the dragon would not listen.

"I'm hungry!" he said. "Feed me."

"Not yet," answered Clarice. "It's not supper time." The dragon became angry and flew to the back of the castle looking for food. His claws tore up the garbage pit, throwing bits of trash and rotten food all over the garden and covering the rose bushes in slop and grime.

But the queen saw this, too, and began to worry that Clarice had overestimated herself. "Two!" she yelled.

Clarice looked at the second mess the dragon had caused and knew that she was close to losing him. But she desperately wanted the dragon to behave so she could prove to her mother that she was fit to be a queen.

"Oh, dragon, won't you be nice? I've promised you all you can eat and a place to live and a comfortable bed."

"But you also promised that you wouldn't hurt me," the dragon laughed. "So there's nothing you can do."

The dragon took to the air again. He flew to the top of the castle and blew smoke down through the chimney.

Billows of black smoke filled the castle, covering everything with a layer of soot. The dragon smiled at what he'd done and felt his prank was very clever.

But the queen was not amused. Standing in a cloud of smoke, she glared at the dragon and yelled, "Three!"

"You can't stop me from being naughty," said the dragon. "You gave your word that you wouldn't hurt me."

"You made a promise, too," Clarice said.

"I had no intention of keeping it," the dragon said, settling on the ground next to her. He mocked her, believing that she was harmless and now he would have the run of the castle. "What are you going to do, chop off my tail?"

The dragon didn't realize that the princess had tricked him. Because the dragon had broken his promise, she had power over him. She wouldn't need a sword or a lance. And she wouldn't need to cut off his tail. She centered her mind so that the intention in her heart was pure because she did not want to act in animosity, anger, or haste.

Then she grabbed him by the tail and called out, "Dragon, dragon, beast of bone! I will turn your tail to stone! If from kindness you do shrink, I will slow you down to think!" The dragon extended his wings and tried to fly but his tail hung down like a weight, and he couldn't rise above the castle tower. He slowly sank onto one of the parapets.

"Now will you stop being naughty?" the princess called to the perched dragon.

"No! Never!" said the dragon. He was growing a little afraid and started to think about being nice, but still his dragon nature made him rebel.

Clarice rushed up the tower and touched the dragon's back wings. "Dragon, dragon, beast of bone!" she said, "I will turn your wings to stone. If from niceness you do shrink, I will slow you down to think!"

He flapped his wings but found they were so stiff and heavy that he couldn't fly at all!

"Now will you stop being naughty?" asked the young princess.

"No, no, no! Never, never, never!" wailed the dragon, but inside his heart he was beginning to think very hard.

Clarice reached out and touched the dragon's front claws and said, "Dragon, dragon, beast of bone! I will turn your claws to stone! If from goodness you do shrink, I will slow you down to think!"

Now the dragon began to panic. He couldn't move his front claws or his wings or his tail. Virtually paralyzed, he began to regret his promise to be nice. But still he cried out, "No, no, no! Never, never, never!" Then he rolled off the tower and down he fell, landing with his snout two feet in the dirt and his rear claws flailing in the air. The princess quickly ran down the stairs and stood before him in the courtyard.

The dragon said something to her, but it was muffled because his face was in the dirt.

"What did you say?" she asked.

Again the dragon mumbled something.

"Excuse me, I can't hear you. Could you say that again?"

The stuck dragon finally managed to say, from the corner of his mouth, "Pull me out! Pull me out!"

The princess stepped beneath the dragon's immobile tail of stone and pulled, until the dragon's snout was freed from the dirt and the beast lay helpless before her.

"Oh, thank you!" said the dragon, as he spit dirt from his mouth. "I've decided that I don't want to be naughty any more. No one can stop a dragon from being naughty—a dragon has to choose it for himself. But for as long as we can remember, every knight and king from far and near has been trying to beat us into being good. They chopped off our tails and cut our wings and clipped our claws; but you didn't, you just slowed me down so I could think about being good."

"Well, I thought!" said the dragon. "I thought and I thought in a way I'd never thought before."

"I can see that it wasn't kind to make the clothes muddy. It wasn't nice to get slop all over the roses. And it wasn't good to blow smoke all through the castle. But when a dragon gets all jazzed up and excited about being mischievous, he has to be slowed down. And now that I'm slowed down, I'm thinking I want to choose to stop making trouble, and choose to be nice instead."

The princess smiled. She looked up at the queen, who was smiling too, proud of her daughter's ingenuity. "Well, I'm sure that the queen will forgive your mischief and let you be my pet dragon if you do three nice things for her."

"I will, if you'll do something with my tail, my wings and my claws," said the dragon. Clarice touched the dragon's tail, wings, and claws and said, "Dragon, Dragon! Beast of wing! Make my mother's heart to sing!"

The dragon lifted himself lightly off the ground and flew to the clothes that he had gotten dirty. He washed them all with the soapy water in the nearby tub and hung them again on the line.

The queen smiled and sang, sweetly and brightly, "One!"

Then the dragon flew to the back of the castle and picked up all the garbage and tidied up the garden. He carefully replanted the uprooted bushes and made sure that everything was clean again.

The queen smiled and sang, sweetly and brightly, "Two!"

Then the dragon flew to a castle window and blew fresh air all through the castle till every last speck of smoke and dust was gone.

The queen smiled down on the dragon and her daughter and sang, "Three!"

She came down into the courtyard and congratulated her daughter. "You proved that you can control the dragon," she said. "So you may keep him for a pet."

Clarice turned to the dragon and thanked him for finally making the choice to be nice.

"Thank you," said the dragon to the queen, "for raising a daughter wise enough to tame a dragon without cutting off his tail and chopping off his wings. That's what all the dragons in the world have been waiting for."

9

The Light of Unity

$\mathscr{F}$or many years, whenever the people in the town of Bickerville had a problem, they drew their inspiration from a book they called *The Philosophy.* In it, everyone said, was the key to happiness and freedom. But instead of being happy and carefree, the faces of the townspeople were drawn and heavy. They were constantly bickering and arguing over the slightest thing, and when they passed their neighbors in the street, they would look away as if they hadn't even seen them. And it was not only the mood of the town that suffered. The town was poor, the buildings old and decrepit, and most of the people didn't seem to know what to do with themselves. They all looked miserable.

"Why is the town so unhappy?" Moriah wondered. She was constantly fighting with her parents and her sisters and brothers and even the girls she felt were her friends. She felt there must be a way out, so she went to her grandmother and asked for her help.

Moriah's grandmother explained how, many years before, the people of the town had been looking for a solution to their problems and when they went in search of an answer, they found *The Philosophy.* Moriah's grandmother had been a young girl when they discovered the ancient book on the shelves of the town's library. Supposedly, those shelves held all the wisdom of the world.

At first only a few people knew about the book and read it, but things seemed to be a bit better for them. They seemed relieved and had less stress. But soon more and more people started to read it and follow its advice. After a few months, there wasn't a single person in the town who didn't follow *The Philosophy.* Everyone felt better about themselves for a little while, but eventually they began to feel worse. But by then no one knew what to do about it.

Fascinated by this bit of history, Moriah began to understand why she always felt so awful, but she didn't yet know what to do about it.

She decided that she needed to venture to the town's library and find the book for herself. Maybe people had simply misunderstood the book and reading it would give her some clues as to how to help the town emerge from its current state.

The library was located in the basement of the town hall, and from the looks of it, not many people had been in it for quite a while. The door slowly creaked open as she moved inside to gaze at all the books—she had never seen so many. The air had a peculiar musty, leathery smell, and there were other old smells she couldn't name. At the front of the library sat an old man, his face gaunt and weary. She greeted the man and asked, "Can you tell me where to find The Philosophy?"

The librarian's face drew tight when he heard the question. He had been working there as the town's librarian since the day the book had first been discovered, and though he felt some guilt about having helped to discover it, he mostly blamed the others for accepting so readily what was inside it without question.

"If I do, you'll just end up blaming me for all the trouble it caused," he said.

"You don't understand," she replied, "I'm trying to find a way to make things better . . . maybe there's something in the book that other people didn't see."

He eyed her warily but saw sincerity in her face and decided to help her. He led her through deep corridors of books where the shelves curved in upon themselves and almost formed arches across the already narrow rows. Finally he brought Moriah to a shelf packed tightly with books. In front of it there was a small wooden pedestal on which the book sat. He motioned to the book and then shuffled back to the front of the library.

She approached the imposing tome. On its cover was a thick layer of dust, which she brushed away to reveal the full title: *The Philosophy of Blame.* From the wear on the cover and the edges of the book, she could see that many people had read it, but now it sat deep underground, gathering dust. Everyone had learned its lessons so well that they no longer needed to consult the book. Its philosophy had become their way of life.

She tried to lift the book but strained under its weight. She relaxed it against its pedestal and it flopped open. She glanced at the first few pages, which explained that the key to problem solving was realizing that you weren't responsible for bad things. If you instead realized that it was other people's fault and blamed them, you could stop worrying.

The author explained his guilt about abandoning his children. He had been in constant emotional pain, but then he had realized that his actions were actually his own father's fault, because his father had abandoned him when he was a child. He also blamed his mother, whose constant criticism while he was growing up had made him doubt himself. He cataloged all of the objects of his blame: his neighbors, strangers, young people, old people. It seemed that nearly everyone in the world had a place on his list of blame.

Moriah understood why the philosophy was such an attractive idea, but she had seen for herself the confusion and problems that following it had caused.

She worried that she would never find an end to all the problems in her lifetime. She only saw a vicious cycle: she would meet other people who would blame her, and she in turn would blame them or someone else, and on and on. This was exactly what had happened to the people in her town. They all said the problem was someone else's fault, but the person they blamed was meanwhile busy assigning blame to them or to whomever they thought was at fault. Everyone said mean and spiteful things to one another, which led to more of the same. If everybody in the whole world blamed everyone else, she thought, nobody would take responsibility for making their own life better. This kept going until every single person in the town blamed someone else for something that had happened, and no one in the town wasn't blamed for something, whether or not they were responsible.

That's why things were so bad—everyone was so busy pointing fingers that laying blame had become the whole town's most consuming interest. This had been going on for so long, everyone had forgotten that any other way was even possible.

But maybe what happened in the past isn't always important, Moriah thought. Maybe this very moment is what's important—whatever I can do right now and in the future. Blame, she realized, didn't solve problems. It just made them last longer.

After several hours of sitting on the floor, poring over the pages of the book in search of an answer, she finished it and closed it. To her dismay, she had found nothing in the book that seemed to solve the dilemma.

She left the book, thanked the librarian, and returned home to think about what she had read.

The next morning she awoke and realized that the only way to get rid of the old philosophy was to find a new one. She would have to go into the library again and search for another book that might help the people of Bickerville.

The librarian wasn't able to be very helpful this time, because it had been so long since anyone had wanted to know about other ways of doing things. He had forgotten many of the titles he kept on his shelves. He simply pointed Moriah in the general direction and left her to it.

She found herself once again at the back of the library, standing in front of *The Philosophy of Blame.* She scanned the shelves in the dim light looking for other titles that sounded more promising.

As she thought and searched, she saw a light near the top of one shelf that seemed to glow from one of the books. As a matter of fact, the entire row of books shone with the same pale light. Curious, she saw that the light was coming from a book titled *The Philosophy of Unity.* She reached up to take it off the shelf, and as she reached, her hand turned as golden as the book. She opened the book to its first page and began to read.

Moriah saw that the book instructed her to have a heart that was kind and radiant. It sounded wonderful, but she couldn't be sure yet whether this really was the answer she had been looking for. She needed to find a way to test whether this new philosophy would actually work.

She took the book to the librarian and asked if she could check it out and take it home with her. But that wasn't all—she tried to see if she could have a radiant heart towards him. She smiled broadly and thanked him for his help. She looked him in the eye and thought that, even though he looked disinterested, she could see the reflection of something more.

She spent the rest of the night devouring the new book. Her whole being was bathed in the bright, golden glow of the words she read. She thought, My heart feels so kind and radiant right now, like there is love pouring out from it.

Her heart certainly hadn't felt that way when she was reading *The Philosophy of Blame.*

The pages of the new book were filled with discussions of qualities such as kindness, mercy, forbearance, forgiveness, consultation. She saw that this was the way everyone in the town could have peaceful hearts and minds. All of these qualities helped to create unity.

The next day she began her plan to show people the new *Philosophy*. It wasn't as easy as she had hoped. When Moriah passed a woman whom she held responsible for the death of her beloved pet rabbit, she felt angry and the radiance she had nurtured the night before dimmed. Thoughts of blame made her mind dizzy, and it was very hard to keep her feelings under control; she found that thoughts of blame and the feelings they led to made reconciliation impossible.

She saw that the reason she was blaming others was because she was busy looking at their faults instead of focusing on their good qualities. Moriah only felt radiant when she was looking at the good in others.

She saw another fellow whom she blamed for making her get sick the previous spring. She was sure he had brought the germs that had infected her. But instead of dwelling on this idea, she thought instead about how kind his face looked, and she flashed him a smile. At first he looked away as usual, but she noticed him peeking at her when he thought she couldn't see him.

The unity was going to be harder and was going to take more effort, she could tell. It meant having to let go of some things that had been important to her. But the warmth she felt as a result made it worth the effort. She didn't want to be separated from her loved ones just because she believed in *The Philosophy of Blame.*

Moriah rushed to tell her grandmother what she had found. She explained what she had learned about *The*

Philosophy of Blame and how it blocks our compassion because we're thinking angry thoughts and blaming others. It's impossible to feel angry and compassionate at the same time. When we feel compassionate love for others, the light of unity burns brighter and solutions are revealed.

She went back to the library, where the row of books was, and asked the librarian to help her bring them out. She clutched an armful of books to her glowing heart.

"What are you going to do with all those books?" the librarian asked.

"I'm going to encourage all my relatives, friends, and neighbors to read them," she answered. And when she emerged from the library, that's what she did. Now that she was learning to control her feelings and focus them in positive ways that led to unity, she finally saw what had been missing in the town. She had the ability to think more clearly and wanted to share what she had learned with everyone.

Once people began to listen to her, some of them felt even worse. They tried to forgive the people around them, but they were still blaming themselves.

Moriah told them they needed to show forbearance to themselves as well.

"My parents blamed others," she told them, "and so I learned to blame myself when something went wrong. If my parents had known about *The Philosophy of Unity,* they would have taught me to solve my problems through unity so that I could respect myself even if I made mistakes."

Soon the new Philosophy began to take hold. People in her family stopped blaming each other. Soon her neighbors stopped blaming each other. After a few months, everyone in the town stopped blaming each other. Eventually the town renamed itself. The name Bickerville didn't seem to fit anymore, and the townspeople came up with a new name: Serenityville.

Because Moriah believed that the light of unity was so powerful that it could illuminate the whole earth, she helped others to believe it too. And because her friends, neighbors, and relatives all believed it, they helped to make it come true.

Part II

Discussion Guide

1

The Legend
of the
Guardians of the Forest:
Effecting Change in
Your Environment

𝒯he story of "The Legend of the Guardians of the Forest" conveys the importance of conserving one of the great natural resources of our planet, the forests, and the critical importance of unity to the success of this endeavor. It deals with the first law of human ecology, which ecologist and microbiologist Garrett Hardin summarized, saying, "we can never do merely one thing." By this he meant "the world is a complex of systems so intricately interconnected that we can seldom be very confident that a proposed intervention in this system of systems will produce the consequences we want."*

The people of the village plan to chop down the ancient forest. The boy in the story had tried to save the forest one hundred years earlier and has actually managed to keep people out of the forest for a period of time, but eventually

---

* Garrett Hardin, "An Ecolate View of the Human Predicament." http://www.garretthardinsociety.org/articles/art_ecolate_view_human_predicament.html, 25 January 2005.

he finds he can't save the forest all by himself. He realizes it's going to take more than one person. When he sends the wind to find a receptive soul, a young girl named Terrah responds to the call. The task of the young girl is first to understand that the forest is a community and then to teach this new understanding to her fellow villagers in a way that will inspire them to preserve the forest. Human beings are part of a community as well, not only amongst themselves, but as part of the entire community of nature. Preserving that community means respecting the different forms of life within it and seeing that each has a role to play, even if it's not apparent to the naked eye.

Because the villagers don't at first see that the trees are important, Terrah needs to show them that the forest helps to preserve their health and quality of life and is not simply a commodity to be used and discarded or consumed for the purpose of gaining wealth. To accomplish this task she makes a noble sacrifice that not only astounds her fellow villagers but also causes them to rethink their plans.

The meaning of true sacrifice is apparent in the following quotation from 'Abdu'l-Bahá, son of the founder of the Bahá'í Faith: "Regarding the statement . . . that man must renounce his own self, the meaning is that he must renounce his inordinate desires, his selfish purposes and the promptings of his human self, and seek out the holy breathings of the spirit, and follow the yearnings of his higher self, and immerse himself in the sea of sacrifice, with his heart fixed upon the beauty of the All-Glorious."*

---

* 'Abdu'l-Bahá, *Selections from the Writings of 'Abdu'l-Bahá* (Wilmette, IL: Bahá'í Publishing Trust, 1997), no. 181.2.

Making a noble sacrifice is different than being a victim. There can be joy in making a sacrifice. Can girls make noble sacrifices? Of course they can. This story illustrates how a young girl did so by following the promptings of her higher self.

Questions for Discussion

1. The Great Tree in the middle of the forest said that there was great treasure in the trees of the forest. What was the treasure?
2. What benefits do trees bring to other life? How are trees like the planet's lungs? Can people survive without them?
3. What did the townspeople want to use the wood for? Is it always wrong to cut down trees?
4. All the insects and animals came to surround the girl when she was in danger. They said, "We are a community. We are not a commodity to be used and discarded. Turn back. Turn back!" What is a commodity? How is it different than a living thing?
5. What saved Terrah from the fate of the Great Tree?
6. How was Terrah a hero?
7. Why had the boy been unable to save the forest?
8. What does the word "sacrifice" mean? How were Terrah's actions sacrificial? How is that different from being a victim?
9. Why must we sacrifice for one another? In what ways can we sacrifice to save the forests of the world? Who would benefit from these sacrifices?

10.   How did Terrah save the boy who was trapped inside the tree? How did he save himself?

11.   What does this story teach us about male and female roles in our culture?

12.   How is the survival of every creature on the planet affected when we chop down a forest? Are there ways to compensate adequately for these effects?

13.   The Bahá'í writings say "every part of the universe is connected with every other part by ties that are very powerful and admit of no imbalance, nor any slackening whatever."* They further state,

> . . . even as the human body in this world, which is outwardly composed of different limbs and organs, is in reality a closely integrated, coherent entity, similarly the structure of the physical world is like unto a single being whose limbs and members are inseparably linked together.
>
> Were one to observe with an eye that discovereth the realities of all things, it would become clear that the greatest relationship that bindeth the world of being together lieth in the range of created things themselves, and that cooperation, mutual aid and reciprocity are essential characteristics in the unified body of the world of being, inasmuch as all created things

---

* 'Abdu'l-Bahá, *Selections from the Writings of 'Abdu'l-Baha* (Wilmette, IL: Bahá'í Publishing Trust, 1997), no. 137.2.

are closely related together and each is influenced by the other or deriveth benefit therefrom, either directly or indirectly.*

14.   What are the implications of the statements above? How do they relate to Garrett Hardin's statement that "we can never do merely one thing"?

15.   Do the forests of the world have "guardians"? Are there spiritual consequences to the decisions we make about how we manage the earth's resources?

---

* 'Abdu'l-Bahá, quoted in Bahá'í International Community, Conservation of the Earth's Resources, 2.1.1. http://bahai-library.com/compilations/conservation.resources.html.

2

The Cave of Whispers: Identity and Community

*M*any women seem to lose their identity—their true self—while they are growing up. Somehow it gets buried or lost in the process of growing up female in a male-dominated world. Instead of developing their true identity, they fabricate something that is not true in an effort to please others. When a person strays from his or her true identity, he or she becomes fearful and powerless, without strong interpersonal boundaries, unable to live heroically.

Identity is one's distinguishing character or personality—that which makes us unique and distinct from others through what we think, feel, desire, and choose. A person's sense of her own identity enables her to realize that she exists as a separate person and that she, as an individual, is valuable because of her unique qualities. To be your true self is to act without hypocrisy or constraint. It is knowing who you are, what is important to you, what you think is right or wrong, and where you fit in the world.

"The Cave of Whispers" tells of a girl named Nedonis who is forced by some dark and troublesome whispers to live in a cave. The whispers have attacked her identity and told her things about herself and about the world around her that aren't true. As a result, Nedonis does not know her own identity. She is passive and lacks willpower, and she has not grown and developed normally. Nedonis is not happy, for she cries when she sees what delightful things lie beyond the cave, but she is too afraid to venture outside. The whispers have distorted her sense of herself, her view of the world, and her understanding of her place in it.

When the wise old woman Sophia becomes aware of Nedonis's situation, she prays for Nedonis to be given the strength to defeat the "ever-present insidious foe" that has, in effect, imprisoned her in the cave. Sophia plays an important role in helping Nedonis find the courage to abandon the whispers and become her true self.

This story illustrates how cultural influences mold and shape girls' identities. Many cultures, including our own, disempower girls and discourage them from exploring their world and taking important risks to grow and develop themselves and their capacities. The story suggests a remedy, though.

One of the main points of the story is that we need other people in our lives. We need to feel connected with others, and we need to participate in a community if we are to develop ourselves fully. An individual cannot fully develop in isolation, separate from the community. Nedonis was unable to believe in herself and couldn't leave the cave or recognize what was best for herself until she found a spiritual mentor who believed in her.

This need for connection and community applies to everyone, both male and female. We can only develop to our fullest potential within the context of a community. We will likely have many mentors in life. They can be anyone— a parent, a friend, a teacher, or anyone else who wants to help strengthen our voice and honor our identity, our skills, our excellence, and our aspirations. A spiritual mentor is someone who will help us discover who we really are and will help us avoid suppressing our true identity and conforming to traditional roles that mold us into what a sexist culture believes we "should" be.

Though many cultural influences can block the development of a girl's true identity, perhaps the most pervasive negative influence today is the inordinate emphasis that is placed on being physically attractive. This emphasis leads many girls to think that their physical appearance determines their value as people. Traditional thinking on self-esteem suggests that this cultural emphasis heavily influences a girl's self-esteem and shapes her self-concept. Although few would suggest that this is a valid measure of any person's worth, our culture communicates that message to girls nonetheless in a multitude of ways. Images in the media of model-thin women and girls who fit the Western cultural ideal of feminine beauty lead girls to compare themselves to the unrealistic ideal and estimate their worth according to how closely they measure up to it. If other influences that would help girls to discover their true identity are lacking during their formative years, then they do not develop strong self-esteem and instead come to believe that their identity and self-worth lie in their physical appearance. As a result, their attention becomes focused on trying to perfect themselves physically to live up to an unrealistic ideal.

The task of developing a healthy identity is further complicated for girls because the forceful and aggressive "masculine" qualities that boys are encouraged to develop are more valued in our culture than are the more nurturing and gentle "feminine" qualities that girls are encouraged to cultivate. Girls are taught to subject their capacities and desires to the male ego. However, the teachings of the Bahá'í Faith turn this dynamic around and provide a new and healthier perspective on the situation:

> The world in the past has been ruled by force, and man has dominated over woman by reason of his more forceful and aggressive qualities both of body and mind. But the balance is already shifting; force is losing its dominance, and mental alertness, intuition, and the spiritual qualities of love and service, in which woman is strong, are gaining ascendancy. Hence the new age will be an age less masculine and more permeated with the feminine ideals, or, to speak more exactly, will be an age in which the masculine and feminine elements of civilization will be more evenly balanced.*

Furthermore, 'Abdu'l-Bahá, the son of the religion's founder, makes it clear that one's true identity and worth have nothing to do with the physical body. He explains, "Man—

---

* 'Abdu'l-Bahá, quoted in J. E. Esslemont, *Bahá'u'lláh and the New Era* (Wilmette, IL: Bahá'í Publishing Trust, 1998), p. 149.

the true man—is soul, not body; though physically man belongs to the animal kingdom, yet his soul lifts him above the rest of creation. Behold how the light of the sun illuminates the world of matter: even so doth the Divine Light shed its rays in the kingdom of the soul. The soul it is which makes the human creature a celestial entity!"* "The Cave of Whispers" underscores the need for connectedness, reminding us that we need unity and community. We cannot learn who we really are, much less become our true self, without participating in a community and without a spiritual mentor. Nedonis was finally able to believe in herself, emerge from the cave, join the community, and develop her gifts because she found a spiritual mentor in Sophia.

Questions for Discussion

1. The whispers are an "ever-present insidious foe." What do they represent?
2. The whispers tell Nedonis things about herself and the world that aren't true. Why does Nedonis accept what the whispers tell her? Why doesn't she question what the whispers say?
3. How do the whispers imprison Nedonis? Why doesn't she just leave the cave?

---

* 'Abdu'l-Bahá, *Paris Talks: Addresses Given by 'Abdu'l-Bahá in 1911* (London: Bahá'í Publishing Trust, 1995), no. 28.6.

4.   What finally enables Nedonis to leave the cave?
5.   How is Sophia a spiritual mentor to Nedonis?
6.   What is the remedy that counteracts the influence
      of the whispers?
7.   How is Nedonis heroic?
8.   How are unconscious cultural influences like the
      whispers in the cave?

3

The Keeper of the Shoes: Being Yourself

$\mathcal{G}$irls are pushed and pulled in the process of growing up in families and in a culture that often expects them to be quiet, obedient, demure, pretty little princesses, without regard to what the girl wants for herself. The discussion of "The Cave of Whispers" talks about the importance of recognizing our spiritual identity and the importance of participating in a community so that we can fully realize our potential. But this is not the end of discovering who we are. Many people in the world show forth spiritual qualities such as love, mercy, justice, and truthfulness, but just because they all have these qualities does not mean they are identical.

A heroic girl can play many roles, all of which complement each other and form a wonderful whole. Each role has its own responsibilities and rewards. Sometimes we choose roles, like the ones for our jobs, but some are established for us, like being a sister or a daughter.

In "The Keeper of the Shoes," Raven imitates the guests at her parents' party simply by stepping into their shoes and seeing what life is like for them. It is natural for children to emulate the adults they see, but imitation can only go so far. There comes a time when you must determine your own identity. It is fine to admire a particular part of another person's life and want to be like them. But in the end everyone is unique and so must discover a unique self.

Raven sees a lot of different things about the guests that she likes, and it's good to try to be like the people we admire. If a person is very kind and generous, then that person will make others feel good just by talking to them and interacting with them. It is perfectly acceptable to say "I want to be kind and generous so that I can make other people feel good." But that does not mean you need to imitate everything else that the person does. Everyone must find their own way to express these qualities. For a doctor, it may be the cheerful way they treat patients. For a teacher, it may be the patience and love they show to their students. Even if the qualities of different people are all the same, people can show them in different ways.

Part of learning about how you will express these spiritual qualities means learning about your natural talents and gifts. Everyone has talents, even if they don't realize them, and through the process of learning about yourself, you can discover all the things that you have to contribute to others. The Bahá'í teachings tells us to regard people as a "mine rich in gems of inestimable value."*

How does a person learn what their own "gems" are? *Being* yourself means first *understanding* yourself. That

---

* Bahá'u'lláh, *Gleanings from the Writings of Bahá'u'lláh* (Wilmette, IL: Bahá'í Publishing, 2005), no. 122.1.

means asking yourself questions: What are the things that you enjoy the most? What are your interests? What do you want to do to make the world a better place? Just like digging gems from a mine, answering these questions and discovering your own "gems" requires effort. It's not likely that you will wake up one morning and suddenly know the answers. Instead, the answers come from investigating the world outside and the world inside ourselves.

The answers are not always the first thing that comes to mind. Sometimes people pretend to like things simply because they are popular or because they think they're doing what other people want them to do. For example, there are certain roles that some people say girls can't fulfill, thinking perhaps they're not smart enough or strong enough. But the reality is that women and men are equal, which means that a girl can do whatever she chooses.

There can also be a lot of different answers to our questions about ourselves, because no one is the same all the time and we are always growing and changing as we go through life. Just like the guests who are more comfortable in mismatched shoes, finding an identity that is true to yourself may not mean fitting into a mold but rather being a person that no one has ever been before.

An essential part of being yourself is to find your unique voice, to speak the truth, and to not let your voice be silenced. The power of speech is essential to the life of the heroic girl. You have a right to speak, to tell others who you are. When you speak your truth out loud, you know yourself better and others get to know you, too.

After sincerely examining the lives of all of her guests, Raven decides that she wants to be herself. One of the important things that she realizes while experimenting with the guests' shoes is that it is difficult to be anybody. Even though the guests are people that Raven admires, they all have worries and doubts. Raven is able to see that there is no perfect way to be. Even though you may be envious of the personality or qualities that others have, it's best to be yourself, to like yourself, to be honest about who you are, and to be confident that others will accept you.

Questions for Discussion

1. What are a few words you can use to describe yourself?
2. What are some of the roles that you have now? Will you always have these roles?
3. In what ways are you unique? In what ways are you like other people?
4. Who are some people in your life that you admire and want to be like?
5. What qualities and attributes would you like to have? What can you do to develop them?
6. What are some ways to learn about yourself?
7. Do you have talents that you keep to yourself? If so, why?
8. Do you know of someone who could use some help discovering their own talents and gifts? What do you think might be helpful? Can you think of any ways that you might help this process?
9. In the story, are some of the guests more important than others?

10. Why are the guests in the story more comfortable in mismatched shoes?

4

The Girl Who Could Open Doors with her Heart: Imaging, Affirmations, and Prayer

*I*n "The Girl Who Could Open Doors with her Heart," King Shevon's negative thoughts and the negative images in his heart bring his entire kingdom close to destruction. It is the king's own words that lock the door to the treasury, and it is his belief that it can't be opened that makes the task of unlocking it impossible. The king's dreams of poverty, disease, and famine become realities, and even though he is creating these realities through his own negative thoughts, he cannot see it.

However, the king's power to destroy the kingdom with his negative thoughts and feelings can be counteracted. Through the pure-hearted advice and assistance of Florence he is able finally to create positive affirmations and replace the negative images in his heart and mind with positive ones. Once he does so, his kingdom is transformed for the better—not only for the king himself but also for all of his citizens.

Though our thoughts and feelings don't become real in exactly the same way that King Shevon's do, they have a very powerful effect on us. If you have to deal with something difficult and you think of it as impossible, you can end up defeating yourself before you even begin. When people look at a difficult task and say "I can't do it," then they begin to create that reality for themselves. But if you believe that you can do it, then seeing it as achievable will inspire you to persevere and look for ways to solve your problem.

One way to think about this is that there are two kinds of vision. One is the vision that's dependent on our eyes and the other is the vision inside our minds—our imagination. When we close our eyes, we can imagine and form images and pictures in our mind. This process is sometimes called "visualizing" or "imaging." The images in our mind are personal, but they are no less real than the world we see with our eyes. Two people can look at the same event or object and perceive it in two completely different ways, thanks to their unique perceptions and the images they create in their mind—that is, the way they interpret it.

Have you ever met someone who seemed to speak negatively about everything? It's very difficult to listen to people who don't have anything positive to say. They give the impression that there is no hope. They are seeing only negative images in their mind's eye.

Speaking positively in the midst of tribulation creates hope in our own hearts and in the hearts of those who are listening. Visualizing the possibility of good things happening to you no matter what may be going on at present is a skill that will help you throughout life, and it is a quality of the heroic female spirit.

Even though we can't make our thoughts materialize the way the king in the story does, we do have the power to change our thinking, which can in turn bring about great change in our lives. There are many things that we can't control, but we do have power over our own perceptions and reactions. In some ways it's as if we each have a kingdom within us. The kingdom is our self-image, our confidence, our hopes and dreams. When we experience difficulties in life, we can visualize something negative in our minds or something positive. By believing in ourselves, having courage, and thinking positively, we fortify our internal kingdom. If we choose instead to focus on negative thoughts that erode our confidence and courage, this reinforces the feeling that we're inadequate and unworthy, which undermines and destroys that kingdom.

Just as the king in the story has a responsibility to protect his kingdom, each of us is responsible for protecting our own internal kingdom through affirmation. You have the power to strengthen or weaken the kingdom that is inside you, depending on whether you keep your mind and heart focused on learning from your experiences and trying to grow as a person. If you take such an approach, then even great difficulties can become positive events.

The concept of looking at life's tests and trials as educational, growth-inducing experiences is found again and again in Bahá'í writings. For example, 'Abdu'l-Bahá writes, "To the loyal soul, a test is but God's grace and favor; for the valiant doth joyously press forward to furious battle on the field of anguish, when the coward, whimpering with fright, will tremble and shake. So too, the proficient student, who hath with great competence mastered his subjects and committed them to memory, will happily exhibit his skills before his examiners on the day of his tests."* To look at tests and trials in this way is not easy and requires constant vigilance, but the rewards are immeasurable.

If we will visualize ourselves as intelligent, creative, capable people, we will have the confidence to pursue all of our goals. Such self-affirmation can also help to draw us closer to God. Prayer and trust in God are vital tools that can be of tremendous benefit and aid to us. If we find ourselves lacking self-esteem, confidence, and optimism, we can ask God for assistance to change our negative thoughts and feelings into positive thoughts and feelings. We can choose to trust in God's wisdom and assume that all of the things we experience in life are ultimately for our own benefit. The following prayer from Bahá'í scripture provides a wonderful example of how we can ask for God's assistance and give ourselves affirmation in the process:

> O God! Refresh and gladden my spirit. Purify my heart. Illumine my powers. I lay all my affairs in Thy hand. Thou art my Guide and my Refuge. I will no longer be sorrowful and grieved; I will be a happy and joyful being. O God! I will no longer be full of anxiety, nor will I let trouble harass me. I will not dwell on the unpleasant things of life.

---

* 'Abdu'l-Bahá, *Selections from the Writings of 'Abdu'l-Bahá* (Wilmette, IL: Bahá'í Publishing Trust, 1997), no. 155.2.

O God! Thou art more friend to me than I am to myself. I dedicate myself to Thee, O Lord.*

As Florence tells King Shevon, merely having these positive thoughts and images in our minds and believing in them isn't enough. We also need to take action. We have to combine the two visions by taking the image that's in our mind and working to make it into the thing that we see with our eyes. As 'Abdu'l-Bahá said, "the power of thought is dependent on its manifestation in deeds."†

If you have an image in your mind of yourself as a kind and generous person, then it's up to you to make sure that vision becomes a reality. If you have an image in your mind of yourself as a hero, then it is up to you to manifest that heroism by helping to make the world a better place.

Questions for Discussion

1.   When things got bad for King Shevon, his attitude made them worse. What could the king have done differently?
2.   What does it mean to have a pure heart?
3.   Does the reason you do something make a difference in the outcome?

---

* 'Abdu'l-Bahá, in Bahá'í Prayers: A Selection of Prayers Revealed by Bahá'u'lláh, the Báb, and 'Abdu'l-Bahá (Wilmette, IL: Bahá'í Publishing Trust, 2002) pp. 174–75.
† 'Abdu'l-Bahá, Paris Talks: Addresses Given by 'Abdu'l-Bahá in 1911 (London: Bahá'í Publishing Trust, 1995), no. 2.6.

4. Are there times when you have faced problems you thought you couldn't overcome? If so, how did you get through them?

5. How does thinking positively about our problems help us to overcome them?

6. What are some challenges that helped you to learn or to grow as a person? Did you think they were a good thing at the time? How can a changed perspective help while we're experiencing challenges?

7. What are some of the mental images you have of yourself? Some of them are probably negative, and some are probably positive. What things must you do to make the positive images of yourself become a reality?

5

The Girl Who Climbed a Ladder to the Stars: Gender Equality as a Prerequisite to Peace

*T*he story of "The Girl Who Climbed a Ladder to the Stars" deals with inequality between the sexes and breaking down the barriers that perpetuate it. Its hero is a young girl named Maya, who goes against the rules of the village of Tambala because she wants to climb a ladder. She has been told that women and girls are to do the cooking, the sewing, the cleaning, and the child care, but they are forbidden to climb ladders. There is a legend connected to the ladder, a prophecy that could someday bring about peace if it were fulfilled. The prophecy is that when someone climbs a ladder to the stars, there will be peace.

Maya strives to develop her individual identity, yet she's forbidden to do the one thing she most longs to do, which is to climb a ladder. One day the urge to try becomes too strong to resist, and she quickly finds herself the object of the village's scorn and ridicule. When Maya loses confidence in herself, Mother Earth encourages her to climb a ladder to the stars and actually helps her do it.

Maya's problem is that she wants to follow her heart and develop all of her unique gifts and powers, but the rules of the village have made her believe she can't and shouldn't. This is similar to the situation of girls and women in many parts of the world today who are taught to believe that only certain paths of endeavor are open to them. When Maya summons the courage to do as her heart tells her, it not only brings her greater personal fulfillment but also enables her to better serve the needs of the village and, indeed, the world.

The need for Maya and all girls and women to develop their unique gifts and capacities is an integral part of achieving world peace. Although bringing an end to armed conflict and violence is a necessary step toward the goal of peace, it isn't enough. It doesn't get at the root causes of war and won't, by itself, create prosperity and justice for all. The teachings of the Bahá'í Faith indicate that achieving true peace will not only mean bringing an end to war as we know it but will also involve eradicating a number of long-standing problems that have plagued humanity throughout history. These include racism and all forms of prejudice, the inordinate disparity between rich and poor, unbridled nationalism, religious strife, lack of education, and inequality between the sexes.*

---

* See *The Promise of World Peace: To the Peoples of the World* (Wilmette, IL: Bahá'í Publishing Trust, 1985), a statement written by the Universal House of Justice, the international governing body of the Bahá'í Faith, in October 1985 and addressed to the peoples of the world.

Bahá'u'lláh, the Founder of the Bahá'í Faith, states, "All should know . . . Women and men have been and will always be equal in the sight of God" and that God regards men and women "on the same plane."* The Bahá'í teachings make it clear that women are to be given equal rights with men and that this action will have practical consequences in all areas of life. However, to achieve this equality requires recognition that every person is endowed with gifts and strengths and that women and girls must be given the opportunity—through education and participation in every area of human endeavor—to develop and exercise those gifts.

'Abdu'l-Bahá, the successor of Bahá'u'lláh, explains that when equality of the sexes is achieved, "Then the world will attain unity and harmony. In past ages humanity has been defective and inefficient because it has been incomplete. War and its ravages have blighted the world; the education of woman will be a mighty step toward its abolition and ending, for she will use her whole influence against war. Woman rears the child and educates the youth to maturity. She will refuse to give her sons for sacrifice upon the field of battle. In truth, she will be the greatest factor in establishing universal peace and international arbitration. Assuredly, woman will abolish warfare among mankind."†

---

* Bahá'u'lláh, in *The Compilation of Compilations Prepared by the Universal House of Justice 1963–1990, Volume II* (Maryborough, Australia: Bahá'í Publications Australia, 1991), no. 2145.

† 'Abdu'l-Bahá, *The Promulgation of Universal Peace: Talks Delivered by 'Abdu'l-Bahá during His Visit to the United States and Canada in 1912*, compiled by Howard MacNutt, 2d ed. (Wilmette, IL: Bahá'í Publishing Trust, 1982), p. 108.

If women are to participate in all areas of human endeavor, then young girls must be educated and urged to develop all of their gifts and strengths so they can be qualified to participate. This can be done by encouraging them to pursue their interests, whatever they may be, and to choose courses of study that will prepare them for careers in law, agriculture, teaching, medicine, science, art, computer technology, parenting, and, in fact, anything that would be of benefit to humankind.

Historically, women have been denied equal rights with men in all parts of the world. It has only been relatively recently, and not even in all parts of the world yet, that this has begun to change. Until this change began, it was generally considered wiser for women not to know how to read or write. They were encouraged to occupy themselves only with drudgery, and they remained ignorant and uneducated. However, today, there is growing recognition that priority must be given to the education of women and girls if it is not possible to educate everyone, since it is through educated mothers that "the benefits of knowledge can be most effectively and rapidly diffused throughout society."* This is the connection between the education of women and children—especially female children—and world peace. Every girl is endowed with gifts that can contribute to the advancement of society, but only if they are developed.

---

* Bahá'u'lláh, *The Kitáb-i-Aqdas: The Most Holy Book* (Wilmette, IL: Bahá'í Publishing Trust, 1993), N76.

Questions for Discussion

1. What was the rationale in the village of Tambala for not allowing girls and women to climb ladders?

2. What did the people of Tambala say to Maya to try to stop her from climbing the ladder? What effect did this have on Maya?

3. Maya had to break away from what the village believed and taught. How did this affect the village? How did this affect Maya?

4. What did Maya learn by making the choice to climb the ladder? What did Maya lose when she climbed the ladder? What did she gain?

5. How is climbing the ladder like getting an education?

6. How was Maya a hero?

7. What kinds of rigid roles did the men and women of Tambala have? Why didn't anyone challenge these roles?

8. Can you think of some women today who have challenged gender roles and accomplished something that usually only men do?

9. In what way was the young man named Phoenix in the story changed? What did he lose in this story? What did he gain?

10. How are the men of Tambala limited by the rigid gender roles?

11. 'Abdu'l-Bahá said, "As long as women are prevented from attaining their highest possibilities, so long will men be unable to achieve the greatness which

might be theirs."* How does Maya's story demon-
strate this concept?

12.   What does the ladder traditionally symbolize?

13.   What kind of virtues would you have to develop to
       bring peace to the world? What virtues did Maya
       and Phoenix develop?

---

* 'Abdu'l-Bahá, *Paris Talks: Addresses Given by 'Abdu'l-Bahá in 1911*
(London: Bahá'í Publishing Trust, 1995), no. 40.33.

6

The Wall of Sorrows: Simple, Heroic Acts of Kindness

*J*ealousy, anger, and violence are just a few of the problems the villagers of Sorrono face in "The Wall of Sorrows." The men are constantly at war with other villages, and the resulting negativity spreads to the women until the villagers are at war with themselves as well. The people of the village wage war because they believe that it will prove their superiority over other villages and people and also because of the treasures they gain from the villages they conquer. But the results of the war don't bring them happiness. Instead, they are saddened by the losses incurred in battle, and the spoils of war arouse jealousy and eventually hatred.

Though the women of Sorrono are not waging the wars, they suffer greatly because of them. For a very long time they have consoled themselves by going to the Wall of Sorrows. This has allowed them to focus on their grief. The wall gives them a place to discharge their sadness, which gives them a measure of relief, but it echoes their sadness and pain so that no one is ever truly comforted. All of the villagers are unhappy and are focused on trying to fill their emotional needs with material things, but nothing seems to satisfy them. There are always more riches to possess and more places to conquer. The villagers' desire for treasures and glory prevents them from seeing that they already possess a treasure that is greater than any other they could hope for: the capacity for kindness.

One girl, Nova, realizes that kindness can save the villagers from destroying themselves. Instead of repeating the messages of hate, envy, anger, and sadness that the villagers have heard over and over again, she shows them that a new message is possible. She demonstrates her bravery by breaking the established pattern and her heroic actions save the village. Because of Nova's initial words of kindness and their positive effect, the other children begin to follow her example, and soon the whole village becomes known not for its greed and aggression but for its kindness.

Everyone in the world, not just the villagers in this story, needs to receive messages of kindness to feel loved and valued. We don't need to wait until there is violence and hate to spread kindness. It's a virtue that is always needed, and there can never be too much of it.

Words of kindness, even though they may appear simple, have tremendous power to restore hope in a world ravaged by materialism, violence, vanity, and war. The Bahá'í writings describe the power of utterance by explaining that "Every word is endowed with a spirit. . . . One word may be likened unto fire, another unto light, and the influence which both exert is manifest in the world."*

------

* Bahá'u'lláh, *Tablets of Bahá'u'lláh revealed after the Kitáb-i-Aqdas,* pocket-size ed. (Wilmette, IL: Bahá'í Publishing Trust, 1988), pp. 172–73.

Choosing to be kind and influencing others with words or acts of kindness is an intrinsic element of the heroic female spirit. This attribute is so important that Bahá'u'lláh says his "first counsel" for us is to "possess a pure, kindly and radiant heart."*

By showing forth a heart that is pure, kindly, and radiant, you can become a hero to the people around you. Even though kindness may not seem like a very heroic thing in itself, its effect is like that of a tiny pebble dropped in a great lake. It creates ripples that can eventually spread much farther than we might have thought. Our emotions affect the people around us, who reflect and often amplify those emotions, much like the wall in the story. If we show sadness, then the people around us are likely to feel sad too. If we are able to present joy and radiance, then they will feel that and can pass it on. When people are treated with kindness, respect, and dignity, they will want to show the same to others.

Treating others with kindness doesn't mean we will never have problems with them, but it does mean that if we have a problem with another person, we will look at them with the eye of kindness. When our hearts are kindly and radiant, we will want to resolve difficulties in a way that isn't hurtful to anyone.

Once the people of the village of Sorrono experience kindness, they feel that all the things they previously thought so important are of far less value to them. This is an important spiritual lesson, and you can help others learn

---

* Bahá'u'lláh, *The Hidden Words* (Wilmette, IL: Bahá'í Publishing, 2002), Arabic, no. 1.

it by making kindness a part of your everyday life. You can be a positive influence on others, not just friends and family, but everyone you meet, wherever you go.

Questions for Discussion

1.   The men of Sorrono think they are superior to the people of other villages. What are some ways that people believe they are superior to others? What effect does this sense of superiority have on others? What does this attitude do to the person who holds it?

2.   If you look at another person with the eye of kindness, will you feel superior to them?

3.   The Wall of Sorrows helps the women of Sorrono find relief from their sadness, but it also makes them dwell on it. What are some other ways to deal with feelings of sadness? Which ways do you think are most helpful? Why?

4.   Do you show a different sort of kindness to friends and family than to people you've only just met or don't know at all? Do you think there should be a difference? Why or why not?

5.   The quotation from the Bahá'í writings about speech and its effects states, "Every word is endowed with a spirit. . . . One word may be likened unto fire, another unto light, and the influence which both exert is manifest in the world." What are some examples of words that are "light"? What are some

examples of words that are "fire"? What are some ways to ensure that our words are "light"?

6. Can you think of a time that someone made you feel good just by being kind? What about a time when someone made you feel bad by being unkind?

7. If someone is showing kindness, how do you recognize it? What kinds of things do they say and do to others?

8. Are there times when it might be unwise to be kind to someone? Why or why not?

9. What are some specific acts of kindness that you can perform in your family, school or place of work, and community?

7

The Quest on the Holy Mountain: The Power of Unity

*I*n the story "The Quest on the Holy Mountain," the kingdom is crumbling and people are suffering from poverty, disease, and widespread confusion. King Sadiki knows that he needs to find a solution to all of his kingdom's ills. He consults counselors and sages, but it is his daughter, Janeal, who suggests that there be a quest to the Holy Mountain to seek answers. The king assembles a group of the strongest, wisest, and most cunning men in the kingdom to carry out his quest, but Janeal must lead them. What she brings to the group is her innocence and pure heart, and it is these qualities that finally allow the group to succeed.

Though the champions—the Knight, the Woodsman, the Poet, the Teacher, the Sage, and the Doctor—all want to help the king, they cannot work together effectively because each is convinced that his way is the best way. Each becomes so wrapped up in his particular path that he cannot see the truth. Each one thinks the others are misguided and wrong, but he is unable to reach the summit alone because he forgets the purpose of the quest and becomes distracted by what he believes to be the right way.

In the end, Janeal has to face the peak alone because all of her companions have let their stubbornness overtake them. It is Janeal's pure heart that finally helps the group achieve unity by showing them the reality of the mountain. She shows them that even though each of their ways seems to be different, they are all parts of the pathway up the Holy Mountain. Individually, none of them is complete. But together the group can cooperate to find the solution. Once they all learn to understand the unity that brings them together, they are able to spread that message throughout the kingdom.

The problems of the kingdom in this story are not all that different from those facing the world today. The need for unity is perhaps the most pressing of all of the world's problems. Without it, no matter how strong, intelligent, or powerful people are, they won't be able to work together. Bahá'u'lláh, the founder of the Bahá'í Faith, wrote about the importance of unity and its enormous power, saying, "So powerful is the light of unity that it can illuminate the whole earth."* Instead of seeing that light, though, many people waste their energy trying to promote one viewpoint as the best and all the others as substandard.

There are many reasons that people are disunified. It can be because of racism or nationalism, differences in socioeconomic status, or perhaps because they disagree

---

* Bahá'u'lláh, *Gleanings from the Writings of Bahá'u'lláh* (Wilmette, IL: Bahá'í Publishing, 2005), no. 132.2.

about politics, or religion, or any number of other things about which they have strong feelings and opinions. Instead of working together to find common answers to the problems that face humanity, people allow these differences to come between them and even to be the source of war and bloodshed.

Some people may fear that unity implies sameness, but this is not the case. Unity doesn't mean that everyone needs to think or believe the same thing. A unified world can still have just as many different viewpoints, ideas, and personalities; however, instead of arguing over which is best and clinging to their personal opinions, everyone is willing to engage in a process of consultation from which the truth can emerge. This process involves sharing different ideas with others, listening with an open mind, and being willing to let go of one's own opinion in the interest of finding the truth.

The heroic female is a world citizen. She can be from any land and any creed, but she believes in the equality of women and men and, indeed, of all people. Furthermore, she believes that all religions should be united because they all worship God.

The ability to see unity in all the diverse populations of the world depends on our perspective. If we believe that skin color is a valid way to judge a person's worth, for example, then we can't be unified with people who are a different color than we are. But if we see that everyone has been created by God and is equal in His eyes, then we can feel unified with them for the sake of God. Many people lack a perspective of unity, though, and become so attached to the surface of things that they cannot see the unity underneath them. The world contains a multitude of different viewpoints and ideologies, but unless everyone makes the effort to find ways to work together in mutual respect and harmony, there is no chance for everyone to progress.

The trend of people has historically been towards greater unity. At first people were organized into families and tribes. Then came villages and towns, then cities and so on. Now there are great nations filled with millions of people, and unions of nations are emerging. Our focus now must be on helping the peoples and nations of the world to realize that we are all members of the same human family. Bahá'u'lláh reminds us of our fundamental unity when he writes, "Since We have created you all from one same substance it is incumbent on you to be even as one soul, to walk with the same feet, eat with the same mouth and dwell in the same land."*

Even with the gradual trend toward increasing levels of unity over time, heroic action is still needed to help people realize their unity with others. There must be courageous and pure-hearted women of insight like Janeal who can burn through the veils that divide people and help them to see that they are all made of a single substance.

---

* Bahá'u'lláh, *The Hidden Words* (Wilmette, IL: Bahá'í Publishing, 2002), Arabic, no. 68.

Questions for Discussion

1.   In the story, the king summons the best and brightest to carry out his quest, yet they are unable to achieve it. What does this imply about scientists and thinkers who are attempting to solve our problems?

2.   What are the heroic attributes that Janeal shows in her quest to reach the summit of the Holy Mountain? Why is she able to reach the summit but not the others?

3.   What does it mean to have a pure heart? Why is that a heroic quality? How can it be cultivated?

4.   What are some of the factors that cause people to be disunified? How can these be counteracted? Can you think of some specific examples of disunity? How might you counteract them?

5.   If you feel there is a lack of unity in a group of people, what steps can you take to help create unity?

6.   Can you think of examples of unity in the natural world—among plants and animals? What does this tell us about the need for unity in the human world?

7.   A person's ideology is their way of looking at the world and deciding what's important. What kind of attitude should we have toward people whose thoughts or ideas are different from ours if we want to create unity?

8.   Bahá'u'lláh speaks of the power of unity. Why is it so powerful? Why is it important for people to understand this?

9.   What happens if people don't achieve unity in their personal relationships? What happens if they do not have unity in their families? How does that differ from what happens when they do achieve unity in their personal relationships and in their families?

10.   What happens when there is disunity among tribes, political parties, religions, or other groups of people? What would it be like if they were to become unified?

11.   What happens when there is disunity among nations? What would it be like if they were to achieve unity?

12.   What are the implications of disunity for our planet? How would the implications for our planet change if we were to achieve unity? What things can you do to make a difference?

8

The Princess and the Troublesome Dragon: Creative, Nonviolent Problem-Solving

*I*n the story of "The Princess and the Troublesome Dragon," Princess Clarice wants to be allowed to have a pet dragon, but the queen is not inclined to permit it at first. The queen knows that dragons can be ill-tempered and dangerous and that they're capable of a lot of destruction. In fact, usually those who keep dragons as pets are mighty warriors who control the dragons by cutting off their tails and wings to tame them. The queen doesn't think it's possible to control a dragon without violence, and she is opposed to this because she believes all creatures to be noble.

The princess is confident that she can make a dragon behave without resorting to violence, but she discovers it is a little more challenging than she expected. She must find a creative way to tame her dragon and make him slow down and think about his choices. Although it might seem easier and more expeditious to beat the dragon into submission, the princess wants him to do the right thing for the right reason. She finds a creative way to immobilize him without hurting him, then allows him to suffer the consequences of his own actions. When the dragon's own mischievousness lands him in the mud and he is unable to pull his snout out by himself, she rescues him. As a result, Princess Clarice wins the dragon's trust, and he quickly realizes that he will be much happier and better off if he chooses to behave appropriately.

In this story the princess and the queen are both heroes for similar reasons. The princess is a hero because she has learned to search for a creative, nonviolent solution to a problem that others have solved with violence. The queen is a hero not only because she has raised her daughter to think independently and use her creativity to solve problems instead of resorting to violence, but also because this goes against the prevailing norm.

There are, of course, countless situations in life where we have the choice either to solve our problems with force and violence or to make an effort to find other, more creative solutions. This is true in interpersonal relationships and in virtually every other social or political context. This applies not only to individuals but also to groups of individuals at every level of organization, from the family to the nation.

It is a truism that violence begets violence. Martin Luther King, Jr., stated this truth more eloquently when he wrote,

The ultimate weakness of violence is that it is a descending spiral, begetting the very thing it seeks to destroy. Instead of diminishing evil, it multiplies it. Through violence you may murder the liar, but you cannot murder the lie, nor establish the truth. Through violence you may murder the hater, but you do not murder hate. In fact, violence merely increases hate. So it goes. Returning violence for violence multiplies violence, adding deeper darkness to a night already devoid of stars. Darkness cannot drive out darkness; only light can do that. Hate cannot drive out hate: only love can do that.*

Decades of research in the social sciences have established that violence is mostly a learned behavior. This is good news, because it means that the descending spiral Dr. King refers to can be broken. Research has also shown that people are capable of learning nonviolent problem-solving skills. We don't have to perpetuate the descending spiral. Instead, we can start an ascending spiral of nonviolence and can contribute to a culture of nonviolence by choosing to solve our problems peacefully.

Even if we find ourselves caught in a spiral of violence and aren't sure how to break it, there is help and hope if we have the desire to change. If we are caught in a cycle of domestic violence, a wide variety of social services and support are available in nearly every community to help both victims and perpetrators of such abuse. If you aren't sure where to turn, start by calling your local crisis line. They can assist you to find the help you need.

If you are already finding creative ways to solve problems peacefully in your own life, you may feel that this is a non-issue for you—that you don't need to worry about it because

---

* Martin Luther King, Jr., *Where Do We Go from Here: Chaos or Community?* (New York: Harper and Row, 1967), pp. 62–63.

it's somebody else's problem. However, there may be other ways you can help to bring about change beyond your family and personal relationships. The Bahá'í International Community points out that "A violent society produces violent families. Just as family violence affects the wider society, a violent society reinforces and even creates a ripe climate for family violence."* This suggests that the violence we see on television, in the movies, on the news, in our neighborhoods and cities, and even in other countries and other parts of the world really should be our concern, for these are among the cultural forces that shape our children and youth and determine the future. If we want to live in a peaceful world, we have to create a culture of nonviolence. This is everyone's business, and we all have a role to play.

Questions for Discussion

1.   Why wouldn't it be more expeditious or effective for Princess Clarisse to beat the dragon into submission?

2.   How do you suppose Princess Clarisse developed the ability to solve her problems creatively without violence?

---

* Bahá'í International Community, 26 May 1994, "Creating Violence-Free Families," a symposium summary report. http://statements.bahai.org/pdf/94-0526.pdf.

3. What would have happened if the princess had tried to control the dragon with violence? How might the dragon have reacted?

4. Why exactly does violence beget violence?

5. Do you think it's possible for nonviolence to beget nonviolence? Can you think of how this might apply to family relationships? To other relationships? To relationships among nations?

6. What are some examples of how family violence affects society?

7. Can you think of examples of how a violent society "reinforces" family violence and creates a climate that is "ripe for family violence"?

8. Do you think violence on television, in the movies, and in other mass media is harmful? Why or why not?

9. What are some ways you can create or enhance a culture of nonviolence in your family? In your neighborhood or city? In your nation? In the world?

10. Are there times when violence is necessary or justified? Why or why not?

9

The Light of Unity: A Philosophy of Loving-Kindness and Compassion

At the beginning of "The Light of Unity," the people in the village of Bickerville live their lives by a code called *The Philosophy of Blame*. Even though the people's lives are unhappy and the village is decrepit, no one stops to consider whether *The Philosophy* might be the source of their problems. That is, not until Moriah begins to ask questions about why everyone seems to be unhappy. The other inhabitants of the village are stuck in their patterns of blame and complaint, but Moriah has a sense that there is a different way for everyone to behave and bravely goes in search of it.

Moriah discovers the origin of *The Philosophy* and discovers that its intent is that everyone should blame each other for anything that's wrong. But discovering the book allows Moriah to easily see what the rest of village is blind to: that the villagers are stuck in their cycle of blame. They will never find a way out through blaming alone, and they will always be unhappy as they continue to live by this moral code.

Inspired to save the village from perpetual unhappiness, Moriah searches for a new philosophy that can replace blame and discovers a book called *The Philosophy of Unity*. She tries its principles, such as kind-heartedness, compassion, and mercy, and sees that they are the solution to end the blame. By bringing the new book to the rest of the people of Bickerville, Moriah heroically helps them to transform themselves into a new village—one full of warmth, compassion, and serenity.

When we have a problem, it's often very easy and tempting to blame someone else for it, just as the people of Bickerville do. Even if it's our own fault, blaming others means telling ourselves that we're not responsible for the problem and so we don't have to do anything to fix it. This not only hurts the person who is being blamed, it also hurts the blamer, who, by choosing to make someone else responsible, gives up the power to grow and make positive changes.

Blame is not always arbitrary. Sometimes bad things that happen are indeed the result of someone else's words or actions, but even then, blame is unhealthy. By fixating on what started the problem, we become stuck in the past. We can't let go and find a way to mend the problem at hand. And we make it worse by alienating another person— someone who just might be able to help us find a solution.

When someone feels blamed, regardless of whether they are responsible, they are likely to become defensive and often angry. The way they defend themselves is often to simply return the blame that they feel has been unfairly aimed at them. As the people in Bickerville found out, it's all too easy for this to expand into an uncontrollable, unending cycle where everyone blames everyone else and the inevitable result is that everyone is bitter and unhappy.

Blaming others also means isolating ourselves because it alienates us from the people on whom we place the blame. Instead of being able to seek help from others for our difficulties, if we blame them it means that we have to face everything on our own. Willingness to forgive allows us to remain engaged with our community and not shut ourselves out from the people around us who care about us and want to help us.

Being able to forgive others and show them compassion and understanding, even when they may have done something to hurt us, can be very difficult. It requires the willingness to look beyond the temporary hurt that we may be feeling and seeing that by blaming we are not reducing the hurt, but only transferring it onto someone else. When we feel hurt, we want to reduce our pain, but blaming only increases and perpetuates the feeling of injury. Then the blamer will end up transferring it back out of resentment, and the temporary hurt that we started with can become a long-standing grudge.

Showing genuine compassion and love to others requires that we look beyond the things that they might have done to hurt us. Just as it's easy for people to return blame to us when we blame them, by forgiving others, it becomes easier for them to extend forgiveness and show compassion and mercy. 'Abdu'l-Bahá gives an indication of how to accomplish this:

Love the creatures for the sake of God and not for themselves. You will never become angry or impatient if you love them for the sake of God. Humanity is not perfect. There are imperfections in every human being, and you will always become unhappy if you look toward the people themselves. But if you look toward God, you will love them and be kind to them, for the world of God is the world of perfection and complete mercy. Therefore, do not look at the shortcomings of anybody; see with the sight of forgiveness.*

Embodying the heroic female spirit means seeing God in all of creation and loving all of creation for the sake of God. It requires that we possess a radiant heart and pure motives and learn to forgive others just as we know that God, in His mercy, forgives us.

Questions for Discussion

1. Even though the people in the village are unhappy, they don't realize that they are choosing to be unhappy. How is their unhappiness a choice? How is your happiness or unhappiness a choice?

---

* 'Abdu'l-Bahá, *The Promulgation of Universal Peace: Talks Delivered by 'Abdu'l-Bahá during His Visit to the United States and Canada in 1912,* compiled by Howard MacNutt, 2d ed. (Wilmette, IL: Bahá'í Publishing Trust, 1982), p. 93.

2. The people of the village have created a culture of blame; they blame others because it's all they know. What does this tell us about following the ways of the past? What does it suggest about the example we are setting with our own actions and behavior?

3. If someone hurts you deliberately, does that mean it's OK to blame them? What will happen if you do? What will happen if you choose to forgive them?

4. Is it possible to blame and forgive at the same time?

5. Moriah discovers her solution to the problem by investigating the origin of people's actions in a book. What are some other ways to find out why people feel or act as they do?

6. What qualities does Moriah exhibit in her search for a solution to the problems in Bickerville?

7. When Moriah first tries *The Philosophy of Unity,* she finds that it's not easy. Why?

8. The problem in Bickerville is a spiritual problem. There are many books that attempt to offer solutions to such problems. What books might you consult when you're looking for answers to spiritual problems?

For more information about the Bahá'í Faith,
or to contact the Bahá'ís near you, visit
http://www.us.bahai.org/
or call
1-800-22-UNITE

Bahá'í Publishing
and the Bahá'í Faith

Bahá'í Publishing produces books based on the teachings of the Bahá'í Faith. Founded nearly 160 years ago, the Bahá'í Faith has spread to some 235 nations and territories and is now accepted by more than five million people. The word "Bahá'í" means "follower of Bahá'u'lláh." Bahá'u'lláh, the founder of the Bahá'í Faith, asserted that he is the Messenger of God for all of humanity in this day. The cornerstone of his teachings is the establishment of the spiritual unity of humankind, which will be achieved by personal transformation and the application of clearly identified spiritual principles. Bahá'ís also believe that there is but one religion and that all the Messengers of God—among them Abraham, Zoroaster, Moses, Krishna, Buddha, Jesus, and Muhammad—have progressively revealed its nature. Together, the world's great religions are expressions of a single, unfolding divine plan. Human beings, not God's Messengers, are the source of religious divisions, prejudices, and hatreds.

The Bahá'í Faith is not a sect or denomination of another religion, nor is it a cult or a social movement. Rather, it is a globally recognized independent world religion founded on new books of scripture revealed by Bahá'u'lláh.

Bahá'í Publishing is an imprint of the National Spiritual Assembly of the Bahá'ís of the United States.

Other Books Available from Bahá'í Publishing

Gleanings from the Writings of Bahá'u'lláh
BY BAHÁ'U'LLÁH
A selection of the most characteristic passages from the outstanding works of the Author of the Bahá'í Revelation

As the youngest of the world's independent religions, the Bahá'í Faith comprises several million adherents who can be found in virtually every part of the planet. Its members represent what may well be the most ethnically and culturally diverse association of people in the world. Its phenomenal expansion since its inception in Persia during the nineteenth century has been fueled by a body of teachings that its followers regard as the Revelation of God's guidance for the collective coming of age of humankind. The source of those teachings is Bahá'u'lláh, the Prophet and Founder of the religion, who left a voluminous body of writings.

Gleanings from the Writings of Bahá'u'lláh is an extremely important compilation that sets out the Bahá'í teachings on a myriad of subjects. Among the themes that fall within its compass are the greatness of the day in which we live, the spiritual requisites of peace and world order, the nature of God and His Prophets, the fulfillment of prophecy, the soul and its immortality, the renewal of civilization, the oneness of the Manifestations of God as agents of one civilizing process, the oneness of humanity, and the purpose of life, to name only a few.

To those who wish to acquire a deeper knowledge and understanding of the Bahá'í Faith, *Gleanings* is a priceless treasury. To the members of the Bahá'í Faith, it has been a familiar companion

for many decades, bringing spiritual fulfillment to countless people throughout the world. This new edition includes paragraph numbering for easy reference and a revised and expanded glossary.
$12.00 / $15.00 CAN
ISBN 10: 1-931847-22-3
ISBN 13: 978-1-931847-22-3

Selected Writings of Bahá'u'lláh

Though most people see the world's religions as separate, unrelated entities, the Bahá'í Faith sees them as stages in a single process. Each represents a new stage in God's progressive revelation of His will for humanity. These successive revelations have always been the true source of moral values, ideals, and standards.

The revelation of Bahá'u'lláh (1817–1892) is the most recent stage in the process. It marks the collective "coming of age" of humanity and lays the moral foundation for a global society.

Bahá'u'lláh is the founder of the Bahá'í Faith, the youngest of the independent world religions. The cornerstone of his teachings is the establishment of the unity of humankind. Bahá'u'lláh taught that there is but one religion and that all the Messengers of God—among them Krishna, Abraham, Moses, Buddha, Jesus, Muhammad—have progressively revealed its nature. Together, the world's great religions are expressions of a single, unfolding divine plan.

Selected Writings of Bahá'u'lláh provides an overview of the Prophet's teachings, including sections on God and His Messengers, the path to God, spiritual aspects of the world civilization described by Bahá'u'lláh, the nature of the human soul and its journey after death, and the renewal of God's covenant with humanity. This volume complements new Bahá'í Publishing editions of Bahá'u'lláh's major works that have appeared in recent years: *Gleanings from the Writings of Bahá'u'lláh* (2005), *The Book of Certitude* (2003), and *The Hidden Words* (2002).
$10.00 / $13.00 CAN
ISBN 10: 1-931847-24-X
ISBN 13: 978-1-931847-24-7

Healing the Wounded Soul

BY PHYLLIS K. PETERSON

A powerful story of courage, hope, and faith that offers encouragement to survivors of childhood sexual abuse and gives important information on prevention for everyone else.

A survivor of six years of childhood sexual abuse, Phyllis Peterson tells her intensely personal story of abuse and the lifelong quest to find healing and wholeness. Her incredible journey is marked by a series of traumas, ongoing therapy, misdiagnoses, reverses, and seemingly overwhelming obstacles to personal development.

Propelled by an unquenchable desire to investigate spiritual truths and bolstered by the discovery of the healing power of her faith, Peterson triumphs by achieving a lasting positive self-image and turning outward to help others. Today her spiritual journey continues to evolve through the teachings of the Bahá'í Faith, her service as a performing artist, and further study of issues of anger and codependency.

Includes comforting extracts from Bahá'í scripture for those who are suffering, dispels myths about child sexual abuse, and provides helpful information on prevention and treatment of childhood sexual abuse.

$14.00 / $17.00 CAN
ISBN 10: 1-931847-25-8
ISBN 13: 978-1-931847-25-4

Hope for a Global Ethic

BY BRIAN D. LEPARD

How can we look with confidence to the future in a world traumatized by terror, war, and human rights violations?

Terrorism. Wars and conflicts. Genocide. Ethnic cleansing. Torture. Oppression of women. Abuse of children. Debilitating poverty. Against this backdrop of the current world scene, Brian D. Lepard suggests that only a global ethic—a shared set of ethical principles—can meet the urgent needs of our troubled global community. But where is the evidence that such an ethic even exists? And where is it to be found?

In this provocative and engaging book, Lepard asserts that there is indeed hope for a global ethic. Surprisingly, the source of that hope is embedded in the scriptures of the various world religions. Reviewing selections from the sacred texts of seven world religions—Hinduism, Judaism, Buddhism, Confucianism, Christianity, Islam, and the Bahá'í Faith—Lepard identifies numerous common ethical principles found in the sacred writings of these faiths. He clearly demonstrates how these shared principles, when put into practice, will help us peacefully solve many problems facing the world that today seem so intractable.

This inspiring and uplifting book will be of interest to anyone who cares about global issues and seeks spiritual guidance from the world's religious traditions.

$14.00 / $17.00 CAN
ISBN 10: 1-931847-20-7
ISBN 13: 978-1-931847-20-9

The Purpose of Physical Reality

BY JOHN S. HATCHER

If human beings are essentially spiritual beings, then what is the purpose of our existence in this physical world?

John Hatcher examines this and other fundamental questions. According to Hatcher, the physical world is like a classroom designed by God to stimulate and nurture our spiritual growth. *The Purpose of Physical Reality* explores the classroom of physical existence and demonstrates how everyday life experiences can lead us to spiritual insights. By viewing this physical existence as a place to learn about spiritual realities, we come to appreciate the overall justice of God's plan and the divine assistance available to unleash human potential. Not only does this concept of physical reality enable us to gain spiritual and intellectual understanding while living on earth, it prepares us for further progress in the life hereafter.

$12.00 / $15.00 CAN
ISBN 10: 1-931847-23-1
ISBN 13: 978-1-931847-23-0

To view our complete catalog, please visit
BahaiBooksUSA.com.